I0760843

KEEP 'EM ROLLING

by the same author

THE BLACK BUCCANEER
RED HORSE HILL
AWAY TO SEA
LUMBERJACK
WHO RIDES IN THE DARK?
T-MODEL TOMMY
BOY WITH A PACK
CLEAR FOR ACTION!
BLUEBERRY MOUNTAIN
SHADOW IN THE PINES
THE SEA SNAKE
THE LONG TRAINS ROLL
JONATHAN GOES WEST
BEHIND THE RANGES
RIVER OF THE WOLVES
CEDAR'S BOY
WHALER 'ROUND THE HORN
BULLDOZER
THE FISH HAWK'S NEST
SPARKPLUG OF THE HORNETS
THE BUCKBOARD STRANGER
GUNS FOR THE SARATOGA
SABRE PILOT
EVERGLADES ADVENTURE
THE COMMODORE'S CUP
THE VOYAGE OF THE JAVELIN
WILD PONY ISLAND
BUFFALO AND BEAVER
SNOW ON BLUEBERRY MOUNTAIN
PHANTOM OF THE BLOCKADE
THE MUDDY ROAD TO GLORY
STRANGER ON BIG HICKORY
A BLOW FOR LIBERTY
TOPSAIL ISLAND TREASURE

Stephen W. Meader

KEEP 'EM ROLLING

Illustrated by Al Savitt

SOUTHERN SKIES

© 1967 STEPHEN W. MEADER
© 2006 SOUTHERN SKIES LLC

All rights reserved

ISBN 978-1-931177- 72-6 cloth
ISBN 978-1-931177- 73-3 paperback

Library of Congress Catalog Card Number: 67-17155

SOUTHERN SKIES

LITTLE ROCK, ARKANSAS

www.southernskies.com

Dedication

The republication of this book is dedicated with love to Maribelle Taylor Matthews—free spirit, true adventurer, sweet soul, ideal mother-in-law—with thanks for 25 wonderful years, by Jerry Atchley

Foreword

This is a story of the long and dangerous journey to Oregon, back in the 1840's. In a sense, it could be called a sequel to my earlier book, *Buffalo and Beaver*. With the days of the mountain trappers nearly past, young Jeff Barlow continues his painting of the West, but now as a scout for a wagon train bound across the Plains and the Rockies. The reader will find a new hero in Dave March, a teen-age pioneer, who is a member of the train.

In movies or television shows, you will rarely see any oxen pulling the prairie schooners. They use horses simply because so few oxen are left in America. Yet the fact is that oxen hauled the wagons over the Oregon Trail in the early days.

I was lucky enough to grow up in the New Hampshire back country, where the strong, slow, gentle beasts did much of the farm and woods work, and I developed a deep respect for their power and endurance.

In *Keep 'Em Rolling*, I have tried to convey the spirit and determination of the "movers" who opened up the Oregon country and made it part of our America. For those who would like to know more about this fascinating period, I suggest that you read *The Oregon Trail* by Francis Parkman and *The Way West* by A. B. Guthrie, Jr.

Stephen W. Meader

One

It was their fifth night out since leaving Independence, and already the train was settling down to some kind of order. The wagons had been pulled into a rough circle on the prairie, the cattle were let out to graze under guard, and the horses were hobbled. Now cook fires were blazing as the womenfolk started preparing supper.

Five days—sixty-seven miles. Not very far if you stopped to remember it was nearly eighteen hundred miles to Oregon. But to Dave March, it seemed like a good start. He took his bullwhip with him and went out by himself a little way south of the camp. If he meant to be an expert driver, he had to keep in practice.

Twenty feet away there was a single flower blooming on a bush. Dropping the lash behind him, he gave the butt a flick with his wrist. The long whip snapped forward like a striking snake, and the knot at the end nipped off the blossom as neatly as a pair of shears. His hand and eye had lost none of their skill, he thought proudly.

At sixteen, Dave was tall and raw-boned. There was no sign yet of his father's massive shoulders, but he hoped to have them, once he had filled out. The long trail to Oregon would help. From all he had heard about it, a boy turned into a man fast on such a journey.

Already, he remembered with a glow, he had seen Indians. They weren't much to look at—just dirty Kaws in old felt hats and blankets. But they were real Indians, and the people in the wagon train had been told to be wary of them. No tribe, the old-timers said, was more skillful, more full of stratagems for stealing than the Kaws. Dave wandered back toward the feeding cattle. It would be a catastrophe if a thieving Indian made off with one of his father's four big oxen. They were the best team in the whole train—matched pairs, so powerful that any two of them could pull the loaded wagon with ease. And Dave had helped break them to the yoke himself when they were yearling steers.

That was long before the Marches had decided to move from their home in Missouri and head for Oregon. But the oxen made the decision easier. If any animals could survive the rugged trail, these could.

The April night was beginning to get chilly as Dave returned to the wagons. They made a pretty sight, with their white tops tinted by the pink glow that came after sunset.

It was a small train—only eleven families and five or six unattached men, some of whom had no wagons. The vehicles were of all sizes and shapes, from ordinary farm carts to specially built prairie schooners, curved at the bottom and high at each end. But all had hoops, covered by canvas tops, and all were loaded with everything they could hold.

The Marches' wagon was a long, flat-bedded, board-sided affair, not fancy but solid. Thomas March had seen to that. He was a good blacksmith, among other things. Back home he had been the town surveyor and cultivated a small sixty-acre farm. But it was the smithy that really kept the family going. Besides the elder Marches and Dave, there were two little sisters, Becky and Patience, so the money earned by shoeing horses came in handy.

An appetizing smell came from the kettles and frying pans inside the circle. As Dave ducked under a wagon tongue and neared his mother's fire, a big hound dog got up and came to lick his hand.

"Well, Jupe," Dave told him, "you look all tuckered out. Twelve miles o' flat prairie trail too much for you? Wait till we get up in the Rockies!"

The hound gave a half-apologetic wag of his tail and flopped down again near the fire.

"No point in faulting him for being tired," Mrs. March said to her son. "You rode part o' the way yourself while Jupe was scouring the prairie, both sides o' the trail. I reckon he made twenty miles or better today."

She stirred the kettle and lifted the spoon to her lips. "Stew's ready," she said. "Get your plate an' eat. Then you can go out on cattle guard an' spell your father, so he can have supper."

Sarah March was a big woman, tall as a man, and when she gave orders, her children obeyed. Dave finished his stew, wiping up the last of the gravy with a piece of bread. It was good—made with onions and potatoes and a fat prairie hen his father had shot. Reluctantly he got up and called Jupe to follow him.

"Better put on a jacket," his mother told him. "It'll get cold mighty soon."

Outside the camp a breeze had sprung up with the setting sun, and though it had been hot all day, the spring night was chilly. The herd of cattle had stopped grazing and drawn together for warmth and company. He could hear them solemnly chewing their cuds. The horses, on the other hand, were still nibbling at the prairie grass, and a few had strayed off to a distance.

Dave found his father and told him supper was ready.

"Good enough," said Thomas March. "I'll come back an' take over 'bout midnight. First thing, though, you'd better take the dog an' drive in those stray horses 'fore it gets dark. I haven't seen any Injuns around, but 'twouldn't hurt to picket 'em inside the circle o' wagons. They've had a fair bait o' grass."

Two of the other men and three boys were also on guard. Sol Jenkins and the two young Beemans were all close to Dave's age.

"Hey, Sol—Larry—Billy," he called. "Come an' help round up the horse herd."

Sol got up, grunting a remonstrance. He was a heavily built youngster, slow and lazy. "Shucks!" he mumbled. "I was just gettin' comfortable."

"Gettin' comfortable!" Larry Beeman jeered. "Why, you been asleep for the last half hour!"

The four youths walked out through the gathering dusk till they were beyond the last horse in the herd.

"Turn him, Jupe," said Dave. "Bring him back home."

The old hound understood the order. He growled once, then took a nip at the horse's heels. Snorting, the animal swung around and started for camp as fast as the hobbles would let him walk. Within fifteen minutes all the horses belonging to the train were inside the wagon ring and picketed. After that Dave went back to watch the cattle while the other boys turned in.

It gave him a fine grown-up feeling of responsibility to be

out there on guard. Though he was some distance from the other men, their voices came to him faintly through the dark. He sat on a stump with Jupe curled up at his feet and stared off into the prairie night.

Big and empty, this Kansas country was. The stars seemed closer, too, but for all their brightness the land lay dim and half seen. The oxen and the few milch cows were only a dark, shadowy mass off there to his right. Somewhere off on the prairie, a coyote howled, and Jupe stirred restlessly.

"Nothing to be scared of, dog," Dave murmured. "Just a little old prairie wolf." Then he remembered that the Indians sometimes signaled each other with coyote calls, and it was his turn to be uneasy. Maybe he should have brought along his gun.

The howl wasn't repeated, and after a while Dave settled back with his thoughts. He recalled the day the train made up, back in Independence, beside the broad Missouri. The eleven families were an oddly assorted lot, no two from the same town. Some, like the Finleys and Callaways, were well-to-do, he reckoned. They had big, expensive rigs, heavily loaded with their belongings. Finley was a merchant and aimed to open a store when they got to Oregon. Callaway, with his courtly manners and well-tailored black coat, was a real Southern planter from Arkansas and traveled with three Negro servants to wait on him and his wife. Why he should be going so far away was something nobody seemed to know.

Most of the homesteaders were about like the Marches—solid folks without much wealth but with enough money and determination to get them to new lands in the great Northwest. The Beemans, Mortensons, Watsons, Jenkinses, Frosts, and Doanes were in that group. And chief among them was Freeman Doane, who had been elected wagon captain. He looked like a natural leader, a stout, upstanding man with a voice that carried well. His brusque manner grated on some, but the real reason he had been chosen was that years before, when he was a shavetail lieutenant in the Illinois militia, he had fought Indians in the Black Hawk War.

Last of all, there were at least two families that Dave regarded as just plain shiftless. Their ramshackle wagons and poor stock were sure to break down on the trail, and they had a swarm of ragged children, all with runny noses. None of the men had ever been able to make a living, and as far as Dave could see, they were just a drawback to the train. They were only there because his parents and a few others had been too tenderhearted to turn them down.

The one thing the train lacked was a guide. By the time they were ready to roll, all the available mountain men had been hired by other outfits. Doane had a map that he said would get them through to Oregon, but some of the other men, Dave knew, were troubled by doubts. Anyhow, there was little that could be done about it. Tomorrow they'd be crossing the Kaw River and really on their way.

At last, after hours of struggle to keep awake, Dave heard his father coming to relieve him.

"Anything out o' the way?" Thomas March asked.

"Not a thing," Dave told him. "Heard a wolf howl a while back, but it was a real one an' no Injun." He yawned. "Guess I'll go get some sleep. 'Night, Dad."

He went stumbling back to the circle of wagons with Jupe at his heels. Everything was quiet except for an occasional snort from the picketed horses. His mother and the two little girls were asleep in the wagon, but Dave had chosen to spread his blankets under it. So far they had had dry weather. He kept a tarpaulin handy, however, in case of rain, and it was now wrapped around his loaded rifle.

He pulled off his boots, folded one blanket into a pillow, and snugged the other one around him. Almost instantly he was asleep.

What wakened him was a sudden movement by Jupe. As Dave raised himself on his elbow, he felt the dog quivering and heard his low growl. Then, when his eyes became fully open, he saw something move, ten yards away, by the black ashes of the cook fire. A crouching figure was picking up the big iron kettle left there after supper.

Dave snatched his rifle out of the tarpaulin, hoping the priming was still good. As he cocked the weapon, he yelled, then raised the muzzle and pulled the trigger. Along with the echoing report came a crash as the kettle was dropped. An Indian, wearing nothing but a breechclout, went loping off and disappeared between two wagons. And instantly the whole camp was in an uproar. Dogs barked, women screamed, and men shouted questions. It took several minutes for the excitement to die down, and by then Thomas March had appeared.

"What happened, Dave?" he asked sternly. "Were you shootin' at shadows?"

Dave pointed to the iron pot lying on its side. "Jupe woke me," he said, "an' there was a sneakin' Injun tryin' to steal Ma's kettle. I fired in the air, an' he ran like a bear was after him."

"Well," said his father with a nod, "I guess that was the way to do. Killin' him might ha' made trouble. I'll see to it your ma keeps her things in the wagon after this."

Before hitch-up time, the next morning, Freeman Doane came over to the Marches' breakfast fire. "I'd been thinking," he said, "of having all dogs shot. Some of the folks don't like 'em an' figure they eat up too much of our supplies. But this dog o' yours has given me an argument in favor of keeping 'em."

Dave's father set down the heavy ox-yoke he had been carrying. "Glad you see it that way," he told the train captain. "There'd have been some real trouble if anybody started shooting dogs—especially this one. I reckon you were lucky we had the horses inside last night, too. If there's one thing those varmints like to steal, it's a good horse."

"Right," said Doane. "Ready to start in half an hour?"

"We'll be ready," March replied. "Come on, Dave. Help your mother gather things up an' load 'em. Then bring up the cattle."

Three of the wagons were drawn by horses, but most of them depended on ox teams. Dave had heard plenty of arguments on both sides. Horses moved faster, it was true, but oxen had more pulling power and more endurance for all-day work. Also they kept up their strength with no food but grass. They were surefooted, too, and folks said that up ahead, in the Rocky Mountains, that would mean a lot.

With Jupe always at his heels, he went out to fetch the March team. The wheelers, Duke and Prince, were red and white, with long, curling horns and thick necks, fitted for the yoke. Their short legs were powerful, their eyes gentle—almost dreamy. And they weighed more than three-quarters of a ton apiece.

Star and Bright, the lead team, were a year younger and not quite so heavily built. In color they were different, too. Bright, the off ox, was piebald black-and-white, while Star was all black, with a big white spot in the middle of his forehead.

The huge animals snatched a final mouthful of grass and

lumbered toward the wagons. With no more than a word of command and a nudge with the butt of the coiled whip, they moved into their proper positions. The yokes were laid across their necks and the bows pegged in place. Then Thomas March lowered the wagon tongue between the wheelers and fastened it to the great ring in the center of the yoke. A chain was run forward from the ring to the lead yoke, and the team stood ready to go.

"You'd better drive first," said Dave's father. "When we get to the river, I'll take over."

He lifted his saddle from the box under the wagon tail and put it on the big bay horse he rode. Several of the other men were already mounted. Up ahead, Freeman Doane lifted his arm and bellowed the call to move—"Wagons, ho!" There was a chorus of cries from the drivers and a crackle of whips.

"Hup, there!" shouted Dave, and the two teams leaned into their yokes. He walked at the left of Duke, the nigh wheeler, his whip uncoiled and hanging loose from his hand. There was no need to use it yet. The oxen were willing, and the ground was fairly level.

Up on the seat in the bow of the wagon, Mrs. March rode, her strong face shaded by her sunbonnet, Becky and Patience snuggling at her side. And old Jupe, the hound, padded soberly along at the rear.

The wagons lined out nicely behind Doane's tall prairie schooner. His horses set a faster pace than the oxen could follow, so it wasn't long before the twelve vehicles were stretched out over a good half mile of prairie.

Dave looked ahead and saw, through the dust of the moving train, a line of cottonwood trees. They were coming to their first river crossing.

Two

The luck had been good so far. No rain had fallen on the emigrants since their last day at Independence, and as a consequence, the water was fairly low in the Kaw. Dave felt a thrill of excitement when they came near enough to see the wide expanse of river.

He had heard it would be easy enough to ford, but it looked deeper than he expected, and there were dark eddies in the faster water near the shore. He wondered if the animals would have to swim.

Down on the bank a white man was shouting an invitation to use the ferry he operated—a big, flat-bottomed affair that would hold one wagon and team. A number of Kaw Indians shuffled about, offering their canoes. Dave saw the leading men of the train consulting together, and after a while his father rode back to the wagon.

"That feller with the ferryboat wants too much money," he said. "Most of us couldn't afford to ride over on his scow, an' it don't look very safe to me anyhow. We aim to ford, if we can find us a spot. Doane's on his way to look, farther up."

Now that his father was there, Dave went to saddle his

own horse. This was a wiry little black Indian pony they had bought in Independence. The dealer swore she was a trained buffalo horse, but there had been no way to prove it. At any rate, "Cinder," as Dave called her, was quick and willing and had good manners.

Dave pulled the cinch tight and was in the act of mounting when he saw a stranger coming toward him. The young man was dressed in worn buckskins and rode a handsome pinto horse. Behind him, on a lead rope, followed a gray mule carrying a pack.

"Howdy," said the newcomer with a grin. "You folks on your way to Oregon?"

"That's right," Dave replied. "You headed that way, too?"

"More or less," the stranger told him. "My name's Jeff Barlow. Is your head man around?"

"Not right now. He's gone off trying to find a fording place. But you could talk to my dad. That's him over by the wagon."

Barlow nodded his thanks, gathered the reins, and rode on. Dave watched as he swung out of the saddle and started talking to Thomas March. There was an easy grace about him, and Dave liked the look of his lean, weather-tanned face. Under his battered old felt hat, his dark hair hung halfway to his shoulders. There was a bedroll tied by thongs to the cantle of his saddle, and the stock of a rifle was visible in a sheath beside the pommel.

Quietly, Dave rode near enough to listen to the conversation.

"Sounds as if you knew the trail," his father was saying. "If you do put in with us, we could use a guide, I reckon."

"I'm not sure I could qualify as a guide," Barlow replied. "But I'd be glad to help any way I can. I've been over this route before, and I'm acquainted with some o' the Indian tribes you're likely to run into. As for supplies, I carry what I need and shoot my own meat. What I do for a living is paint pictures—Indians, trappers, buffalo, and all kinds of animals. If I ride along with you, I'd like to make sketches of a typical wagon train. Then when I go home to St. Louis, I'll finish 'em up in color. There's a good market just now for paintings that show the West as it really is."

Thomas March looked surprised. "Guess I never met a genuwine artist before," he said with a grin. "O' course, I can't speak for Cap'n Doane, but I'm pretty sure we'd be glad to have you travel with us."

"Good," said Barlow heartily. "I think I'll ride on and see if I can find the captain. As I remember it, the best fording place is less than a mile upriver."

Only half an hour passed before he returned, in company with Doane and a couple of other men. The wagon captain waved an arm and shouted for attention.

"All right, folks—get ready to roll!" he ordered. "We've got a place to cross. You men that don't have wagons, go trail the stock after us. Once the wagons are over, the loose cattle will have to swim for it. You'll want to be mounted when you herd 'em across."

Nervous drivers climbed into their wagons and whipped up the teams, moving on in a cloud of dust. Dave knew his duty lay with the loose stock, and he rode back to take his position in the rear. His father was driving the wagon.

It took time and hard work to get the train across the Kaw. There were deep spots where the oxen had to swim, snorting with terror, while the drivers urged them on with whip and voice. Some of the lower-slung wagons had to be buoyed up with logs lashed to their sides to keep their contents dry. Noon was past before the last wheels had trundled up the farther bank.

Then it was the turn of the herdsmen. Whooping and waving their hats, they drove the spare horses and oxen and the few milk cows into the water, then spurred their mounts in after them. The day was hot, and the cool river felt good to Dave's feet. Then it was up to his knees, and finally to his waist, as Cinder struck out strongly in the deepest part. He had put his rifle and powder in the wagon to keep them dry.

At last the crossing was over. They had made it without losing a single animal or an article of furniture from the wagons, and Dave felt proud of himself and the train. Now, he thought, he could call himself a real "mover"—an "Oregon man."

The train followed the north bank of the river for seven or eight miles before making camp. There was good grass there in the bottomlands, and once again the cattle were turned out to feed while the horses were carefully picketed. That night, as Dave paced back and forth on watch, he was glad to see a tall figure come up to join him.

"Nice spring night," said Jeff Barlow. "Mind if I help stand guard?"

"Gosh, no!" said Dave. "'Course not. It gets sort o' lonesome when I'm by myself."

They sat down on the grass, and the young painter took a pipe from his pocket, filled it with tobacco, and struck a light with flint and steel.

"I remember my first crossing of the Kaw," he said, puffing contentedly. "I was just about your age, and I was headed for the beaver country in the Rockies."

"You mean you went alone?" asked Dave.

"Shucks, no! My dad was a mountain man, and there were

two other experienced winterers in our party. One was an old-timer called Wind River Slim, who taught me just about all I know about the mountains."

"What happened?" asked Dave. "Did you really camp out all through the winter?"

"Snug as you please." Barlow chuckled. "We'd found a nice valley, way up beyond the Sweetwater, an' it was plumb full o' beaver. We caught so many of 'em our horses could hardly carry out the fur in the spring."

"Gosh!" Dave murmured in awe. "But Injuns—you said you knew a lot o' tribes?"

"Well, I made friends with a young Crow chief on that trip, an' later we had a couple o' fights with the Cheyenne. Since then, over the years, I've been all up an' down the country, from the Mississippi to the Yellowstone. I've lived in Sioux tepees and hunted with Pawnees—even got to know some Shoshonis and Blackfeet. Some day I hope you'll see some of the Indian pictures I've painted."

"I wish I could," Dave replied. "But even watching you make sketches would be 'most as good. Maybe you'll do a picture of our wagon an' the oxen."

Jeff Barlow laughed. "Sure I will. Tomorrow, if there's time. I might even draw the old hound here. What's his name?"

"That's Jupe—short for Jupiter. We've had him since I was just a little tad, but he's still a good hunter, 'specially on coons. He's a good watchdog, too."

He went on to tell about chasing off the Indian the previous night, emphasizing the fact that it was Jupe who gave the alarm.

The artist reached down and scratched the hound behind the ears. "Yes," he said, "I can see he's a first-class dog."

* * *

The weather stayed fair, and the train was rolling early the next day. They struck off northwestward across untraveled prairie, broken here and there by clumps of woods. Dave, trailing after the wagons with the loose cattle, saw little of his new friend till evening. Barlow had left his mule with the train and ridden off alone to scout the land ahead.

They made a good, solid twenty-four miles that day and camped by a little stream in a grove of cottonwoods. Just as the supper fires were being started, the pinto pony came into view, and across its rump lay the carcass of a good-sized buck deer.

"Meat, ho!" Barlow called cheerfully. "Everybody come an' get some for the pot!"

At once he dismounted, pulled the deer to the ground, and began skinning. With a sharp knife and deft hands, he had the hide off in a matter of minutes and was cutting up the meat for the waiting hands of the women. Fresh meat was a treat they already appreciated after a week of salt pork.

Dave stood by and admired the way his friend worked. "Where'd you shoot the buck, Mr. Barlow?" he asked.

"Now, look," the man answered with a chuckle. "My name's Jeff, an' you'd better drop the 'Mister.' I was out a few miles ahead o' the train an' came to a little draw full o' brush an' trees. It looked like good deer cover, so I tethered the horse an' went in on foot. Sure enough, this fellow was coming down to the water to drink, an' I got in a lucky shot that dropped him. That's about all there was to it."

"I had a look at your rifle, Jeff," Dave said. "It must be old, with that long barrel, but you sure know how to use it."

"I've had it quite a few years. It's a real Kentucky piece, and my father bought it for me in St. Louis when we were starting our trip to the mountains. I guess I'm used to it. Takes a little longer to load, but for shooting true, I'd rather have it than one o' those new breech-loading carbines. Anyhow, it's traveled a mighty lot o' miles with me, and I don't aim to change."

Their talk was interrupted by the approach of Freeman Doane.

"Well, Barlow," he inquired importantly, "what are things like west o' here?"

"All quiet," said the scout. "We ought to reach the Big Blue day after tomorrow. It's only thirty miles—a fairly easy two days' march."

Another voice broke in from behind them. "Ain't much chance o' makin' it," said little Mr. Peck in his usual whine. "The Skellys' team an' mine's got sore feet. Had to drive 'em too fur yesterday an' today."

Doane frowned. "Oxen, eh?" he commented. "Take a whole day to get 'em rested an' fit to travel. Were they shod?"

"Never heard o' shoeing oxen where we come from," said Peck with a shrug. "We didn't think it was needful."

"Well, go talk to Mr. March, the blacksmith. See if he can fix your cattle up by noon tomorrow. If you two can't keep up, we may have to leave you behind."

Peck slunk off in the direction of the Marches' wagon, and Dave followed him.

"Maybe Pa could set up the forge tonight," he told the unfortunate little man. "I'll ask him, an' you go bring in your cattle, one at a time."

Thomas March looked disgusted when he heard the news. "I can do it, I reckon," he told his son, "but it'll take a good part o' the night. Here, help me get out the tools."

The forge was a light sheet-iron affair, carried in the rear of the wagon. In addition, there was an anvil, hammers, iron strips used for shoe stock, and two barrels of charcoal. By the time they had the coals hot, Skelly arrived with his first ox, and the smith set to work.

Skelly was tall and thin with a dejected stoop to his shoulders. Like Peck, he talked mostly about his bad luck. It made Dave sick to listen to him, but he kept busy working the bellows while his father shaped a shoe. The cheerful clang of the sledge on hot iron helped to drown out the whining voice.

The steer was as sorry a sight as its owner—a gaunt, narrow-chested animal that had been in poor shape to start with. The cloven hoofs were splayed and cracked. Thomas March had to treat them with tar before he could fit the shoes, and it was nearly seven by the time the beast was shod.

Dave's mother came to tell them the supper of venison stew was getting cold, and they knocked off for a quick meal. When they started work again, half the people in the train had gathered to watch, and Dave could hear whispered comments, none of them complimentary to the Pecks and Skellys. Meanwhile, the smith kept at it steadily, his quick, powerful hands shaping and nailing the shoes with surprising speed. It was shortly after midnight when the job was finished and the last lean ox was driven back to the herd.

"Leave the forge right where it is," Thomas March told his son. "It has to cool off 'fore we can pack it. You get to bed now. I reckon neither of us is expected to stand watch tonight."

"All right, Pa," said Dave. "But who's going to pay you for all that work. I don't believe those two fellers have got a dime between 'em."

"Hmph!" his father snorted. "You're probably right. But I didn't do it for them. It was to keep the wagons movin'."

Three

They rested the teams for two days before crossing the Big Blue. Jeff Barlow had warned that they would encounter hard going and scant grass on the haul to the Platte, and it would be well to have the cattle and horses in good condition.

The first day of idleness was a Sunday, and though there was no minister with the train, the movers held a kind of service, with hymn-singing and a few prayers. On the following morning, Jeff dropped by the March wagon and invited Dave to go with him on a hunt.

It was a hot day, and clouds were building up in the west. They rode their sweating horses a few miles out on the prairie before any game was sighted. Then Jeff's keen eyes spotted some moving dots in the distance.

"Antelope," he said. "No use chasing 'em on horseback—they're too fast. We'll go on afoot."

They hobbled the ponies and left them to graze. After half a mile of stalking, Jeff motioned to his companion and they sat down, screened by a patch of buffalo grass and sage. So far the animals had not taken alarm.

"Only way to get in range of an antelope," the painter-scout remarked, "is to make him come to you. Let me have that black hat o' yours."

He placed the hat on the muzzle of his rifle and lifted it high, waving it slowly back and forth. For a minute or two nothing happened. Then Dave saw one of the graceful animals raise its head and start toward them in a series of nervous jumps and hesitations.

Jeff chuckled. "Don't move," he said. "Let him worry a bit longer. He won't be happy till he knows what this thing is."

The antelope continued to approach until at last Dave figured it was about two hundred yards away. Still too far for an accurate shot, he thought. But Jeff was lowering the old Kentucky rifle. He took a slow aim, squeezed the trigger, and right after the report the antelope leaped in the air.

"Got him," said Jeff. "Let's go see."

"Boy!" Dave exclaimed. "I'd have been willing to bet it couldn't be done!"

They found the dead pronghorn crumpled in the grass, a bullet hole drilled in its white chest just below the dark stripe. It looked pitifully small—about half the size it had appeared in life.

"To bad to kill such a pretty thing," said Jeff. "He won't weigh more'n fifty pounds, so there'll only be a bite o' meat for each family."

He swung the limp body over his shoulder and led the way back to the horses. The only other game they brought in was a pair of prairie chickens, one of which fell to Dave's rifle.

The storm that had been threatening all day hit them that afternoon with rolling, crashing thunder and lightning all over the sky. The wind came in gusts that nearly tore the canvas off the wagon tops, but very little rain fell. As a consequence, there was no floodwater in the Big Blue after the storm passed, and they made their crossing without trouble.

A short distance beyond the ford, the train reached the north bank of the Little Blue, and it was alongside this stream that the trail led. Now, Jeff Barlow warned them, they were in Pawnee country. The Pawnees were a warlike tribe, very different from the cowardly Kaws, so the guards were doubled every night, and none of the men and boys got much sleep.

Three days and some fifty miles beyond the Big Blue, Larry Beeman came down with some kind of illness that none of the movers recognized. His fever was high every evening and went down again after sunrise, but through the nights he really suffered. Calomel and other household remedies were of little avail. It was Jeff Barlow who brought the youngster back to health with an herb he had learned how to use when he lived among the Sioux. But though the fever was gone, Jeff insisted that Larry should ride in the wagon and get more rest.

Dave missed him, for they had often shared guard duty. On the second night of his illness, however, a slender figure came toward him through the dusk, and he recognized Lucy Beeman, Larry's fifteen-year-old sister. She was carrying a shotgun and wearing a dark dress that was difficult to see at night.

"Don't mind if I join you, do you?" she asked calmly. "Dad says I'm a better shot than young Bill, so I'd better take Larry's place. Have you seen any Injuns?"

Dave got up awkwardly. "Not a one," he answered. "An' I'm glad to have company, Lucy. Find a comfortable spot to sit, if you can. These hummocks o' buffalo grass aren't the softest stuff in the world."

"Don't worry about me." She laughed and sat down beside him. "What would you do if a whole passel of Injuns came galloping up?"

"I'd probably fire one shot an' run," he told her. "But it isn't very likely to happen. One or two Injuns may come sneakin' around at night to steal stock, but war parties don't generally attack before daybreak."

"Why's that?" asked Lucy.

"I don't rightly know. We could ask Jeff, though. Here he is now."

The buckskin-clad artist came out of the darkness and squatted on his heels. "What's that you wanted to know?" he asked, and Dave told him.

"It's a superstition they have," Jeff answered. "A warrior who gets killed at night can't find his way to the Happy Hunting Grounds—or so they think. But I've heard o' some raids they made at night, an' there'd probably be more if they thought the enemy was asleep."

Lucy thanked him. "Back in Ohio, where we come from, folks don't know much about Injuns," she said. "You lived farther west, didn't you, Dave?"

"Northern Missouri," he told her. "Just about as civilized as Ohio. Once we get to Oregon, though, we'll all be pioneers together. That's about as far west as you can get!"

Jeff soon left them, moving on to make his rounds of the camp. But Lucy stayed till midnight, when Thomas March came to take over the guard duty. Dave liked her. She talked sense—about horses and guns and the Oregon Trail—no silly girl stuff.

* * *

The train was twenty-nine days out of Independence when they sighted the barren sand hills that guarded the south bank of the Platte. They looked like small mountains after the long days on the flat prairie. The "Coast of the Platte" was what old-timers called the ridge of dunes, Jeff Barlow told Dave.

They passed through a gap in the sand hills, and there before them lay the river—a big river, almost like the Missouri. It was wide and muddy, and beyond it stretched a vast, desolate country, so tremendous in its emptiness it was almost frightening.

That feeling didn't last long, for there was too much to do. They made camp on a low bluff above the river, and the stock was taken down to water. Then the boys tried to find wood for cooking fires. Other trains that had come before them had chopped down the few small trees, and the only wood available was such drift logs and branches as had been washed up by spring floods.

The river water itself was thick with mud. After it settled, it was barely drinkable, but it didn't taste so bad when it was used for coffee or tea. What bothered the women was that clothes couldn't be washed.

The trail led up the Platte, following the south bank below the sand hills. All the wagon teams had toughened now. There was no more trouble with the oxen's feet, and the horses suffered only from occasional harness galls. However, there seemed to be less grass the farther they went, and all the animals looked half-starved.

"How long does this last?" Doane asked Jeff Barlow. "We're going to lose some stock if we can't feed 'em."

"Well," the guide replied, "it's near a hundred miles to the next good stream—five or six days at the least. Just have to grin an' bear it, I reckon. One reason the grass is so poor is that buffalo have been through here. Lots of buffalo signs around, but the herd's moved on."

Dave had good reason to know that buffalo had passed that way. In the absence of firewood, he and the other boys were sent out to pick up buffalo "chips," as the dry dung was called. Actually, it made pretty good fuel, burning cleanly, with little smoke and practically no odor. But that didn't soothe the pride of the young frontiersmen.

The extra-strong guard at night was still maintained, though Jeff assured them that the Pawnees were probably following the buffalo, somewhere to the north.

"What makes you think the buffalo have crossed the river?" Dave asked his friend one evening.

"Just a slim hunch that they've moved over, looking for grass," Jeff replied. "The heat bothers 'em, too, so they sometimes head north late in May. Nobody ever knows what buffalo'll do, though. Even the Indians' medicine men have trouble guessing where to find the herds."

"Gee!" said Dave. "I sure hope we run across a few of 'em. Every chip I pick up makes me keener to kill a buffalo!"

Jeff chuckled. "No need to take it so hard," he said. "The first time I came up this way, I was the only boy in the party. I bet I gathered ten thousand of 'em!"

Off to the east they heard a long, quavering howl. It was deeper and more mournful than the coyote's cry that Dave now knew well.

"Buffalo wolf," said Jeff. "They're big an' mean. Strong enough to pull down a steer. We'd better herd the cattle in closer."

As they set out to circle the grazing animals, there came another sound—a terrified lowing that was suddenly cut off. Jeff started running in that direction, with Dave at his heels. After a hundred yards or so, they caught sight of a dark heap on the prairie and another shadowy form loping off into the dunes.

"It's that old cow o' Beemans'!" Dave said, panting. "She was weak, anyhow, an' the wolf killed her easy. See that? Tore her throat right out!"

Jeff nodded. He was looking around as if searching for something. "Want to kill that lobo wolf?" he asked. "My guess is he'll be back here before long. We didn't give him a chance at the meat, and he's probably hungry. Soon as we've driven the other cattle in closer to camp, what say we come back an' take cover behind that clump o' sagebrush?"

Dave, of course, was enthusiastic about the plan. It took only a few minutes to round up the oxen and cows and push them back toward the wagons. Then they checked the priming of their rifles and moved quietly eastward in the darkness.

"Wind's coming from him to us," Jeff whispered. "Unless he sees us or hears us, he won't know we're around."

They lay down on their stomachs behind the sagebrush and watched the cow's body as vigilantly as possible. Even so, the approach of the wolf was so stealthy that neither of them knew it was there till they saw its shape crouching over the carcass. It looked gigantic—twice as big as old Jupe, Dave thought.

He started to cock his rifle, but Jeff's gesture stopped him. The older hunter laid a finger to his lips, indicating they should wait in silence, and after a moment Dave saw why. The wolf looked about warily, then crouched again to tear at the cow's bloody throat. Only when the brute was absorbed in its feast did Jeff pull back the hammer and take aim. At a nod from him, Dave followed suit, and it appeared that the wolf had not heard the two clicks.

"Go ahead—shoot!" Jeff whispered, and with his heart in his mouth, the boy pulled the trigger. At the crack of the rifle, the lobo leaped up from its feast, but before it could escape, Jeff's Kentucky gun also barked. The two shots were less than a second apart.

"Got him," said the scout calmly, scrambling to his feet. "I wouldn't be surprised if both shots landed."

They advanced cautiously, Jeff reloading his rifle as he walked. But no third shot was needed. The animal lay where it had fallen, its great teeth bared in a ghastly snarl. At that moment the moon broke through and shone on the wolf's fur, so pale a gray it looked almost white.

"Yep," Jeff commented, "that's a real lobo—a buffalo wolf—the biggest kind there is. Looks like your bullet broke his shoulder, an' I reckon mine got him through the heart."

"Will more of 'em come?" Dave asked with a shiver. "I thought they ran in packs."

"Not the lobos. Sometimes there's a pair, but mostly they hunt alone. This one's too big to carry without a horse, so if you want to show him off, you'd better go fetch your pony."

"I don't care about that," Dave told him. "But I'd sure like his hide. Think you could skin him by moonlight?"

The sound of shots had been heard by the other guards, and now they came running. Lucy Beeman was among them. When she saw the body of the cow, Dave saw a look of consternation on her face.

"Is—is it our old Blackie?" she asked, her voice breaking in a sob. "Oh, why did she stray so far!"

"My fault, I guess," Dave answered. "I should have seen her quicker an' driven her back. But we did kill the wolf. I'll give you the hide if you'd like it."

"No," she told him with a shudder. "I couldn't bear to touch it. Poor old Blackie!"

As she stumbled away, Jeff patted Dave on the shoulder. "Don't let it fret you," he said. "Taking the blame for something you couldn't have helped was generous enough, an' offering to give her the wolfskin, too. But the way she feels right now, generosity isn't the answer. Give her time. She'll get over it."

With that advice he turned to skinning the wolf. In Indian fashion he left the head on the hide, and when Dave started to carry it back to camp, he found the whole thing weighed close to forty pounds. He was so proud of their kill, however, that he didn't mind the load.

The next morning, when he spread the wolfskin on the ground beside the wagon, Jupe retreated growling and hid under the front wheels. The other boys in camp came to stare in awe at the great, grinning head and the gray-white pelt. But Mrs. March's reaction was different.

"Dave," she said, "if you're bound to keep that smelly thing, you'll have to find your own place for it. One thing sure—it's not coming in my wagon."

The train had to wait till noon that day while repairs were made on two of the wheels of Pecks' rickety wagon. The jolting had loosened the tires, and Thomas March had to get out the forge again to tighten them. What he did was heat the iron hoops red-hot to expand them, hammer them on the wooden wheel rims, and plunge them smoking into the river to cool and shrink. The rest of the movers used the time to make their own minor repairs. The tar buckets were brought from under the wagon tails, and axles were smeared with tar. By the time they had eaten their midday meal, all the vehicles were in shape to move. And meanwhile, to Dave's delight, Jeff had scraped and cleaned the wolfskin.

"All right!" Doane bellowed from the head of the train. "Let's get 'em rolling!"

Dave uncoiled the bullwhip and sent the lash snapping out over the backs of the patient oxen. "Hup, there, you Star an' Bright!" he yelled. "You've had your rest. Now pull for Oregon!"

Four

The days were hot now—blazing hot with a glare of sun reflected from the white alkali dust. Trailing along behind the loose cattle, Dave found the stifling clouds of that dust the hardest thing he had to bear. It got into his nostrils and stung his eyes and covered his face with a gritty white mask.

The horses that pulled Doanes' and Finleys' and Callaways' wagons were still in the lead, where they didn't have to breathe so much dust, but they were slower now. At the start they had been grain-fed and eager. But with the oats used up, they had to depend on grazing, like the other animals, and the frequent stops their drivers made were more for the horses' sakes than to let the oxen catch up. Their ribs showed, and when they stood at rest, their heads hung down.

Up the Platte, day after weary day, the train plodded on. It wasn't just the animals that suffered. There was no more chatter among the women who walked beside the wagons, for they wore handkerchiefs over their mouths to keep out the dust. With the day's end, when they circled for camp, people seemed to come to life once more in the cool of the evening. A banjo strummed, and Dave could hear occasional laughter. It was a good thing, he thought, that humans had the ability to forget their discomforts. He wondered if the cattle felt that same relief as they searched for scanty spears of grass or lay down to rest.

Good water was short, too. More than once they had to make a dry camp, when the trail ran along steep bluffs back from the river. Then a small quantity was portioned out to each thirsty animal, and children cried because they weren't allowed an extra cup at bedtime. The water barrels, lashed to the sides of each wagon, gave off a hollow sound when a hand was struck against them.

There were evidences along the way that other trains had found the going hard. Often Dave would see a bleached ox skull by the trail or a wagon wheel broken beyond repairing. At other places, where a steep climb had to be made, heavy articles had been thrown out to lighten the load. Iron stoves lay there rusting, and once there was a fine mahogany sideboard that must have cost some woman a broken heart when it was left behind.

As a scout should, Jeff Barlow rode far out ahead of the train each day. On the seventh of June, Dave saw him hurrying back, his horse in a lather, and heard him yell in triumph: "Buffalo! Big herd of 'em a dozen miles west!"

It was then a little past noon. At once four men took rifles and mounted their horses. Thomas March was one of them.

"Dad!" Dave cried. "Can't I go? Ma can drive the oxen, an' you know I'm a good shot."

His father turned to the scout. "What do you say?" he asked. "Think he can handle it?"

Jeff nodded. "He's probably worth more on this hunt than he would be guarding the train. Let him come."

They rode northwestward for more than an hour, not moving too fast, for they had to keep their horses fresh. Dave ranged his black mare alongside Jeff's pinto.

"What's the best place to hit a buffalo?" he asked.

"The heart," Jeff told him. "A head shot's no good—skull's too thick. There's a spot just back o' the left foreleg where most o' the hair's worn off. It shows white when the buffalo's running. You put a bullet there an' you've got yourself a cow. Don't fool around with the bulls—their meat's too tough, except the young ones. But when you've got a nice fat cow in your sights, bring your pony up the left an' let her have it."

"Thanks," said Dave. "I'll try to remember if I'm not too rattled. I see you've got a bow and arrows. Is that what you're going to use?"

"Sure," Jeff replied. "Reloading a rifle takes time. With a bow you can shoot oftener an' hit 'em oftener, if you know how. Look—see the dust up ahead? That's the herd."

The great gray cloud came from somewhere inland, beyond the sand hills, and Jeff spurred forward to lead the other horsemen over the rise. As soon as they passed the crest, Dave saw a sight that took his breath away. For miles, actually farther than the eye could reach, the plain was black with buffalo. There must have been thousands—perhaps millions for all he could tell—and the noise they made was like the roar of a giant waterfall. It was made up of the lowing of cows and calves and the hoarse bellow of bulls.

Dave clutched his rifle and urged Cinder into action. The other hunters were slightly ahead, but the black pony sped after them, snorting as she caught the heavy odor of the herd. In less than a minute, the riders were among the fringing outer guard of bulls. Cinder dodged through, avoiding the great shaggy heads and thrusting horns.

He felt a quick glow of pride in his little mare, but there

was no time to think about it. Already he could hear the crack of rifles ahead. The cows were moving now at an awkward gallop, the thunder of their hoofs shaking the prairie. He picked out one that ran just behind the close-packed mass and guided the pony up beside her, twisting in the saddle to bring his rifle to bear. There was the light-colored spot just behind her left foreleg, just as Jeff had described it. He fired when he was less than five yards away and saw the cow stumble, pitching forward on her knees.

Exultantly Dave urged the pony on, trying to reload his rifle as he rode. But he was destined to shoot no more buffalo that day. As the herd rumbled away, he saw the men of the train riding back in his direction. Five dead cows lay there in the settling dust, pathetic brown hummocks on the prairie. Two of them, he saw, had the shafts of arrows through their hearts, and Jeff Barlow was already at work on one of them with his skinning knife.

"Pretty good day's work," he commented as Dave rode up. "How'd you make out?"

"I got one," Dave told him proudly. "She's back there a ways. I guess we'll have plenty o' meat for a spell."

Thomas March had killed a cow, and Finley had accounted for one. Doane, with one of the new-fangled breech-loading carbines, had fired several shots without inflicting a mortal wound. As a consequence he was in a bad humor and critical of the other men's butchering.

At last Dave's father stood up, wiping his bloody hands on his bandanna. "Cap'n," he said evenly, "if you've got nothin' else to do, why don't you pack some o' this meat back to the train? I reckon the womenfolks'll be mighty glad to see you."

The wagon captain's face reddened for an instant. Then he took the suggestion without arguing and loaded some of the

choicest meat, rolled up in a buffalo hide, across the rump of his fidgety horse.

"You're right," he said as he swung into the saddle. "No telling what's happened while we've been up here. I'd better get back and take charge."

Jeff Barlow grinned a little as he finished skinning his second cow. "Well, Dave," he said, "what say we find that critter you've been braggin' about. That is, if she hasn't walked off by now."

He led the heavily loaded pinto back to the carcass Dave showed him. The bulls had scattered and disappeared long before, and the lone cow lay where she had fallen.

"Nice shot," the ex-mountain man remarked. "Square in the heart. But I reckon some credit ought to go to that black pony. How much'll you take for her?"

"She's not for sale," Dave told him stoutly, and Jeff chuckled.

"I figured not," he replied. "A real buffalo horse isn't come by easy."

There was a feast in camp that night. For the first time Dave tasted buffalo tongue, hump meat, and spareribs and found them doubly delicious because he had had a share in providing them. The smell of the roasting meat drifted over the prairie, and Dave wondered why it didn't set the wolves and coyotes howling. Then he remembered that they were having their own feast up above, where the half-stripped carcasses lay.

Jeff must have read his thoughts. "We won't have any trouble with varmints tonight," he said. "They're fed full. But that doesn't make the cattle any less hungry. We've got to get 'em to some grass soon."

The wagons were just being hitched up next morning when

two big prairie schooners came into view. Each was pulled by four horses, and a dozen spare horses were led behind. The vehicles went past at a smart trot, their drivers yelling derisive words at the ox teams. A few women and children could be seen in the wagons, and two mounted men rode alongside.

Dave's father looked after them and shook his head. "Mighty small train for wild country," he said. "They're movin' fast right now, but I wonder how long they'll last once they get into the mountains."

Jeff Barlow had gone out scouting the trail ahead, and when he returned at noon, he also had something to say.

"There's always a few cocky ones," he remarked, "who think they can beat everybody else to Oregon, just by having good horses. I wouldn't want to be in their shoes today, though. I cut the trail of an Indian hunting party headed north."

Doane called a sort of council of war when he heard that. An Indian attack was what all the wagon trains feared most, and none of the men felt like joking about it. They accepted Jeff Barlow's suggestions and the captain's orders without question.

That night they camped in a flat, open area, close to the river. The wagons were pulled into a close circle—"forted up," as Jeff called it—and the horses brought inside. Extra guards watched over the grazing cattle and kept them close. All were keyed to wakefulness, and Dave was alert at the slightest sound. However, the dark hours passed without incident, and though the men were heavy-eyed, they were ready to roll in the morning.

Sometime in the middle of the afternoon, the lookouts who rode in front of the train reported smoke ahead. And half an hour later they came upon a scene that Dave would never forget. The two huge wagons that had passed them so gaily lay overturned and smashed, with fire still smoldering among their contents. Lying on the prairie near them were a dozen mutilated bodies—six men, two women, and four small children—all pierced by arrows and all scalped. The horses were gone, along with the rifles, pistols, powder, and bullets.

Jeff examined the bodies, checked the ground for traces of the attackers, then cast about in several directions. Meanwhile, the women and some of the men pushed on till they were out of sight of the scene of the massacre.

"I figure it was a band of Ogallala Sioux," the scout reported. "Looked like their arrows, anyhow. About forty warriors coming down from across the Platte. No squaws or baggage along, so they weren't just out to hunt buffalo. I'd say the party was young braves, on a raid down here into Crow country to take some scalps. Running across the wagons may ha' been pure luck, an' the sight o' those fine horses was more'n they could resist."

"Well," said Doane soberly, "we've got to bury those people. It's too bad we can't send back word to the settlements, but I don't know how it's possible."

"Maybe we'll run into a trapper packing his furs down to St. Louis," Jeff replied. "Any idea who those folks were?"

Most of the men shook their heads, but Callaway spoke up unexpectedly.

"Yes," he said. "One of them was Pierre Larue, from New Orleans. I met him at a party once in Natchez. A gentleman, certainly, but a bit reckless, I'd judge."

Sadly and silently, the burial detail did its work. The last body to be laid in the long grave was that of a little girl of five or six, most of her yellow hair torn away to leave a ghastly mass of blood and bone. Dave thought of his own small sisters and could stand no more. He went off a few steps and was violently sick.

This tragedy had a deep effect on the people of the train. There was no more singing around the campfires, and on the trail the men huddled close to their wagons, guns always in their hands and eyes searching every hill and gully. It seemed to Dave that the women—his mother especially—showed more courage and good sense than the men. True, they were extra watchful of their children, but the cooking and other household duties were done without complaining.

Jeff Barlow ranged ahead and on both flanks, riding three or four times the distance covered by the wagons. After a day or two they passed the fork of the river and followed the South Platte toward Big Spring—the promised land for which they had been yearning.

It was everything Jeff had described and more. There was clear, fresh water in plenty, not only for watering the stock but also for washing clothes and even bathing. The spring, and the stream that flowed out of it, lay in a narrow valley where the grass grew lush and cottonwoods gave welcome shade from the hot sun.

All the men in the train agreed that they should rest here for two days, to let the half-starved animals regain some strength. When they asked Jeff's advice, he approved. Some of the hardest going east of the Divide lay ahead of them, he warned. And the likelihood of an Indian attack was less because they were now nearer Fort Laramie. Let the cattle and horses feed, he suggested, and spend the time putting the wagons in good condition.

That, of course, meant more work for the blacksmith. The first day Dave pumped the bellows of the forge from dawn till dark. But on the second morning, his father told him to take a break.

"Do anything you like," he said, "but be back here by noon."

What Dave wanted was to go hunting with his friend, the scout. Jeff had done a lot of sketching the previous day, and he, too, was ready to ride. They loaded their rifles, caught and saddled their horses, and were soon out on the prairie, following a ravine that led back toward a range of higher hills.

"Might get us an antelope," Jeff remarked, "or even a stray buffalo. If we do see one, though, it'll be a tough old bull, left behind by the herd. Keep watch for anything that moves."

Five

The hunters had ridden a mile or two when they came to a wider place in the ravine, where water glinted through a grove of trees.

"Must be another spring," said Jeff. "Let's go quiet."

When they reached the edge of the wooded area, they dismounted and tied their horses to branches. Then, motioning again for silence, Jeff led the way in among the trees. Dave could see a pretty little pool ahead, and it looked so inviting that he almost wished he could strip and take a swim. But the idea was suddenly interrupted.

His companion stopped in his tracks, then crouched low behind a bushy thicket. Dave saw him raise an arm to point cautiously forward. Then he lifted his rifle. Drinking there at the edge of the pool was a blacktail doe, her head bent to the water and her big ears twitching nervously.

With the utmost care, Jeff cocked the long Kentucky gun. At the clicking sound, the deer raised her head quickly, sniffing the air. Dave expected to see her bound away before his companion could fire, but Jeff's trigger was quick. At the crack of the rifle, the doe dropped where she stood.

"Couldn't very well miss, at that range." The artist chuckled. "She ought to give everybody a nice change from dried buffalo meat."

He skinned the deer and rolled the venison in her hide. As soon as it was fastened behind the pinto's saddle, they set out again.

Here in the high country the air was clear as crystal. Beyond the first range of hills, Dave could see much bigger mountains lifting dark against the sky. They looked so close that he thought he could reach them in an hour's ride and suggested it to Jeff.

"Distances fool you out here," his friend replied. "Those peaks are in the Laramies, a couple o' hundred miles from here. We'll be seeing all the mountains you're likely to want in the next month."

Soon Jeff decided it was time to circle back. Dave, riding a few paces ahead, chanced to look off to the south and hastily reined in his pony.

"What are those little black specks moving down yonder?" he asked. "Think they could be buffalo?"

Jeff took a careful look. "No," he said soberly, "it's a band of Indians. If we stick to the hollows, maybe they won't spot us."

He took the lead now, picking a northward route that avoided the ridges. Worried, Dave followed, glancing often over his shoulder. After what he had seen a few days earlier, he no longer thought of Indians as romantic figures. Even the word gave him a sinking feeling.

"Come on, boy," Jeff told him. "Don't get jumpy. We'll be back in camp in another five minutes."

The naked prairie opened up before them, and there lay the valley, the cottonwoods, the gray canvas wagon tops. The scout rode at once to Doane's wagon and reported what they had seen.

"There's still three hours of daylight," he said. "My advice is to gather the stock, fill the water barrels, an' haul out o' here. If there's an attack, we could fight 'em off better with the open prairie around us. Too many trees here to give 'em cover."

Doane made some objections but finally agreed to call the men into council. They all voted to follow Barlow's suggestion, and for the next hour they worked furiously, packing the wagons and filling the barrels with fresh water. Then the teams were hitched up, and they lined out, crossing the ford over the South Platte and heading northwest. At sundown the wagons were drawn into a tight circle on an area of flat prairie.

"Now," said Jeff, "it's all right to go ahead with supper. Here's some deer meat for everybody. Just keep your fires small, and don't anyone stray off from camp. All the guns should be ready—loaded an' primed. If any Injuns feel like attacking us, I'm pretty sure we can handle 'em."

In the face of danger, Dave was glad to see that every man in the train seemed to trust the scout's judgment. They brought all the horses inside the circle and kept the cattle closer than usual, under a strong watch.

As darkness fell over the prairie, the guards were tense and quiet. No boy or man wanted to be alone that night. Dave, rifle in hand, was squatting on his heels, watching the skyline, when he was joined by another silent figure. It was one of Callaway's servants, he saw—a big, powerful Negro who went by the name of Abraham. Dave had stood guard with him before and found him a good companion—not talkative but making sense when he did speak.

"Gittin' colder," he whispered as he crouched by Dave's side. "You figger they'll be comin' tonight?"

"Not before dawn, I reckon. Our job is just to keep the cattle in close an' warn the camp if any Injuns do show up."

The Negro nodded and was quiet for a while. Then he shivered and shifted his weight. "No wolves yappin' tonight," he said. "Mebbe a bad sign."

Dave, too, had wondered why the coyotes should be so silent.

"Abe," he whispered, changing the subject, "you think you'll like it way up in Oregon?"

"I'm goin' to like bein' free," the man replied. "Marse Callaway done promise he set me free if I he'p him git to Oregon."

Dave's curiosity was aroused. "I can't figure why he wants to go there," he said. "Wasn't he a rich planter with a fine home?"

Abraham hesitated before answering. "I wouldn't tell most folks," he murmured. "But I know you's a close-mouf' boy. Hit's true. Marse Callaway had a mighty good plantation, with a big house an' more'n two hundred field hands. Then two bad things happens. First off, he gits to gamblin' an' loses mos' all his money. An' after that a young scamp from Vicksburg comes sashayin' aroun' the Mist'ess. They's a duel, an' Marse Callaway shoots him daid. But the man he done kilt was a nephew o' the Governor's, so the state gits too hot to live in. An' here we is."

"Thanks, Abe," said Dave. "You didn't have to tell me, but it won't go any further. And I'm glad you're going to be free."

Toward midnight they heard a wolf howl out on the prairie, and both grinned with relief. Not long after that the second shift of guards came out to take their places, and they walked back to the wagons together.

Dave thought about Abe's story before he went to sleep. Gambling and dueling were a long way from his own experience, but he could feel the tragedy of the Callaways' flight to Oregon. Mrs. Callaway rarely showed herself among the other women, and on the few occasions he had seen her, the rich clothes she wore looked out of place. Nevertheless, he realized she was beautiful in a sad, romantic way. He was sorry for them all.

* * *

The train got under way early the next morning. By the time the heat began to beat down, they had made half a dozen miles, and the wagons were allowed to stop for a short rest. It was while they were standing there, strung out in line, that Dave looked back and saw three mounted Indians approaching. He knew better than to set up an outcry. Instead, he hurried over to tell Jeff Barlow, who had just ridden in from his usual morning exploration.

"It's all right, Dave," said the scout quietly. "I saw 'em, an' they don't look as if they mean any trouble. I'll just ride out an' palaver with 'em."

The whole train was aware of the visitors by now. The men stood uneasily by their wagons, and the women hushed their children. All eyes were on Barlow as he rode his pinto horse out to meet the trio of Indians. Hardly had he reached them when they saw him lean forward to grasp the hand of the one in the middle—an imposing-looking warrior wearing a great eagle-feather bonnet. Even though the meeting took place a hundred yards away, Dave could see that all four appeared relaxed and friendly.

After three or four minutes, the principal Indian raised his

arm in farewell, wheeled his pony, and rode away, followed by his two companions. Jeff returned to the wagon train at a brisk trot.

"Put up your guns," he called. "Everything's fine. That was an old friend o' mine—a Crow chief called Running Wolf. His band's out after buffalo an' headed the same way we are. When we camp tonight, he wants to pay us a visit, along with some of his head men. So we'd better be ready with a few trade knives an' beads an' such for presents. Tobacco, too. They'll want to smoke with us."

The people of the train were cheered by this good news, and the wagons were soon rolling again. Dave saw Jeff mount once more and ride off ahead, this time leading his pack mule. He was sure that the scout was going for another hunt, but this time there was no chance of going with him. Thomas March had given his son the task of driving the oxen.

All the rest of the day, as he plodded through the heat and dust beside Duke, the nigh wheel-ox, Dave watched the prairie. He was hoping for another glimpse of the tall Crow chief in his war bonnet. But the Indians didn't come into view. They must, he decided, be off searching for game.

About four o'clock, when the tired drivers and their families were thinking of making camp, Jeff Barlow came riding down the rocky side of a mesa at their left. There was something bulky tied behind his saddle, and the mule was heavily loaded, as well.

"Got a buffalo!" Jeff called. "Meat enough for a feast."

As they gathered around him, he explained that he had sighted a small herd several miles south of the trail. The fat cow he had killed would provide meat for a day or two, at least.

"There's a little creek ahead," the scout added. "We can be there in half an hour an' have a better place to camp."

The creek turned out to be little more than a dry stream bed with occasional pools of muddy water. It was fit to drink, however, and after buckets had been filled for cooking, the animals were allowed to slake their thirst.

Dave and the other boys went up and down the creek bed, picking up all the driftwood they could find. Soon the fires had been started, and chunks of buffalo meat were sizzling on the spits. The smell of the roasts drifted through the camp, and Dave could understand why old Jupe's tail was quivering with anticipation. His own mouth was watering.

At that moment a commotion was heard on the outskirts of the camp. Looking that way, Dave saw half a dozen Indians in full regalia, approaching on horseback. Without haste they dismounted, tethered their ponies, and entered the circle of wagons.

Jeff Barlow walked over to meet them, his right arm lifted in greeting. The leader of the group was the same warrior Dave had seen earlier—Chief Running Wolf. Now, however, his face was daubed with lines and circles of red paint that gave him a strange, ferocious look. Some of the smaller children started to whimper and were sternly quieted by their mothers.

The scout led the way to the central campfire and motioned to the guests to be seated. As they took their places in a half circle, Dave had a better look at them. All wore eagle-feather headdresses, though none were as elaborate as the chief's. Their faces, too, were painted and as expressionless as though they had been carved from wood.

Jeff moved to the buffalo haunch roasting over the fire.

Drawing his hunting knife, he cut large chunks of meat and handed them one by one to the squatting Indians. There were satisfied grunts as they attacked the dripping meat with their teeth, but no words that could be interpreted as thanks.

"Go ahead, folks," Jeff said to the onlookers. "Eat your own supper. This'll take time."

The families returned to their individual fires and began the meal, though there were few among them who didn't keep an eye on their visitors.

"Hmph," Thomas March grunted under his breath. "Good thing that was a big cow he brought in. I was afraid we'd go hungry with those savages comin' to supper."

When the Indians had had second helpings and each had belched comfortably, Jeff took a pipe from what he called his "possible sack" and filled it with a rank mixture of tobacco and *shongsasha*, the bark of the red willow. With a burning stick from the fire, he lighted the pipe, took a long, slow puff, then passed it ceremoniously to Running Wolf. It was smoked by each of the Indians in turn before it was handed back to the young scout.

At that point Jeff rose and said a few words in the Crow tongue, emphasizing what must have been a welcome with sign language.

The chief replied, his deep, gruff voice rolling out words that had a friendly sound, even though they couldn't be understood.

Next, Barlow led Doane forward, somewhat against his will. The wagon captain was introduced as a chief, with the appropriate gestures, and then Dave heard Jeff tell him in a low voice that it was time to bring out the presents.

Awkwardly, Freeman Doane reached in his pockets and fished out several knives, along with two or three twists of black tobacco. The scout added a small bag of vermilion, the red powder that was prized by the Indians. All these articles were laid before the chief, who grunted and passed them along to his companions. Dave noticed that he kept the best articles for himself.

There followed a brief speech of thanks, another round of puffs at the pipe, and at last the Indians rose with dignity to stalk back to their horses. When they had gone, Doane wanted to know what all the palaver had been about.

"How'd you know they were friendly," he demanded, "when they were all in war paint like that?"

Jeff grinned. "That vermilion paint is just for dress-up," he replied. "War paint is black. Anyhow, I've known Running Wolf since we were both youngsters. Didn't I tell you he was a friend o' mine? We're invited to hunt buffalo with 'em tomorrow an' visit their camp in the evening."

Doane was inclined to fume about losing another day, but Jeff talked him out of it.

"You're ahead o' schedule now," he said. "A day's rest'll do the critters good an' give the ladies a chance to wash an' mend clothes. Besides, we'll get more meat to take with us if we find the main herd."

The other men chimed in with words of agreement, and it was soon decided that they should accept the Crows' invitation. Dave went to sleep that night with his head full of the coming buffalo hunt.

Six

They saddled their horses in the chilly half-dark before daybreak—six of the best shots in the train. The fact that Dave was allowed to ride with them made him proud. It was Jeff Barlow himself who had urged that he be included.

Two miles south of the camp, they sighted a line of moving specks on the crest of a distant ridge.

"Buffalo!" cried several of the hunters, but Jeff corrected them.

"That's Running Wolf an' his braves," he said. "They're quartering this way, an' we'll meet up with 'em before long."

There were some twenty men in the Indian hunting party. As they drew near, Dave saw that they no longer wore the ceremonial feather bonnets. Each brave was stripped to a loincloth and moccasins, his long black hair hanging to his shoulders, and each carried a hunting bow and arrows. A single eagle feather was thrust into the chief's headband.

"How!" called Running Wolf, lifting an arm in greeting. Then he said a few guttural words to Barlow and pointed westward.

"Come on!" the scout told the white men. "The herd's over yonder."

The cavalcade rode forward at a walk, keeping to the low ground. Far ahead a lone Indian was gesturing toward a deep draw that came down out of the hills on their left. It was up this ravine that they moved in single file. The unshod Crow ponies made no noise, while the shoes of the white hunters' horses clinked occasionally on stones. As they neared the crest, Dave saw an Indian scout dismount and creep upward to look out over the high prairie.

There was no question about what he had seen. Scrambling down again, he leaped astride his pony, and all the Indians rode after him over the top. The scent of buffalo must have been in the air, for Dave's little black mare sprang forward without urging and took him out of the ravine right behind Jeff's pinto.

The herd was less than half a mile away. Although the Indians were racing toward it at a dead run, the buffalo hadn't started to move as yet. But the bulls on guard were bellowing their warning, and by the time the riders reached the outskirts of the herd, cows and calves were galloping off to the southward.

Dave had begun to feel like an old hand at the business. He chose his cow, then let the mare bring him alongside. At his shot the big animal stumbled a few strides and dropped. A few yards away, Jeff had also brought one down. He reined in his pony and rode back to join Dave.

"Nice shooting, boy," he called. "I reckon I've had enough. How about you?"

"Sure," said Dave. "If everybody gets one, we'll have more'n we can carry."

Oddly enough, he realized, his desire for killing was gone.

Looking off across the prairie, he could see the buffalo herd fleeing before the Indians in a vast cloud of dust. But nearer, the ground was dotted with dark lumps. Crow arrows and white men's bullets must have accounted for close to thirty buffalo.

While the skinning proceeded, Dave was sent back to the train to bring more horses. At the same time, a number of squaws and extra ponies appeared from the Crow camp. The meat was cut up, rolled in the hides, and loaded on the pack animals. And before noon all the hunters had returned.

Many of the emigrant women came from farms, where they were familiar with ways of curing meat. Nearly every wagon carried barrels of salt, and some of it was used that afternoon to preserve part of the drying buffalo meat. Slabs of the flesh were laid out on rocks in the sun, while the younger children kept the flies off with sagebrush switches.

As sunset neared, Jeff Barlow went from wagon to wagon, speaking to some of the men. With Doane's approval, he was choosing those who should represent the train at the Crow encampment that evening. When he came to talk to Thomas March, Dave stood as close as he dared.

"We'll leave enough men here to guard the camp," the scout was explaining. "But we ought to make a decent showing over there. Steady folks who'll know how to behave."

"Gee—could I go?" Dave begged. "I'll be quiet. Won't even smile!"

"This is business for men," his father replied sternly. "You aren't old enough."

"Wait a bit," Jeff put in. "I was just about to ask if he could come. I wasn't any older when I first met Running Wolf at a parley like this. As a matter o' fact, he likes the boy. Told me today he looked like a smart hunter. So I sort o' figure he ought to be along."

Dave had sense enough to keep still while his father considered the matter. But when the older man finally nodded, he was almost beside himself with joy.

There were seven in the party that rode eastward to the camp of the Crows. As they drew near, Dave saw the cluster of tepees, pale in the dusk. There were more of them than he expected, and they had been pitched in a sort of ring. In the middle a fire blazed, and squaws and children were sitting about it, gnawing at buffalo bones. When the white men were within a hundred yards, a chorus of yapping dogs announced their coming.

At first Dave thought the camp was unguarded till he saw four mounted braves ride in from various directions. One of them must have been hidden beside the trail as they passed.

As if by magic, the women and children disappeared into the lodges. Running Wolf, with a group of elders of the tribe, stood by the fire to greet the visitors. After he and Jeff had exchanged greetings, all the men, white and red, sat down in a circle and the ceremonial pipe was lighted. Dave took a modest place behind his father.

This time it was not Running Wolf who opened the speaking but a much older Indian. He rose with dignity and stood erect, his white hair hanging on either side of his gaunt, wrinkled face. He wore no war bonnet, but a pair of polished buffalo horns, mounted on a beaded band, adorned his head. And in his right hand he held a tall lance, from which a dozen scalps dangled. The old warrior was more than six feet in height, and Dave thought he had never seen a more impressive figure. As he learned when Jeff replied to his speech, the man was

White Calf, great chief of the Crow nation and the father of Running Wolf.

While the ceremonies were going on, Dave's eyes were busy studying the Indian camp. The lodges, he could see, were made of tanned and bleached buffalo hides, sewn together with thongs. Each had a flap-protected opening at the top, to let the smoke out, and a doorway covered by a leather curtain. From the nearer tepees the brown faces of squaws and children peeped out as they watched the proceedings. Up to eight or ten years old, the children went stark naked. The women wore a variety of clothing, all the way from blankets or cheap calico, bought at the trading posts, to really beautiful garments of white doeskin.

Once more gifts were laid before the chief, and this time the Crows responded with presents of beaver pelts, stone pipes, and bear-claw necklaces. Then the two companies parted in friendship, and the whites rode back to their wagons.

Dave was chuckling. "Don't know what Ma's going to say when she sees me with these big bear claws 'round my neck. I reckon I won't want to wear 'em much anyhow—they sort o' scratch. But I'm sure proud to own 'em."

"They're 'bout as much use as this pipe I got," his father replied with a grin. "The thing's so heavy in the bowl, it takes both hands to hold her."

* * *

After a night's camp at Ash Hollow, the train labored on up the Platte. The trail was rougher now, and the craggy hills crowded them closer to the river. There was so little grass that all the stock—horses and cattle alike—were gaunt with hunger. Each morning as Dave yoked the sad-eyed oxen, he noticed how their ribs and hip bones stuck out. But they still pulled willingly.

The two milk cows were in almost equally poor condition, and it was hard to get enough milk from both of them to feed Becky and Patience. The only four-footed dependent of the March family that seemed to stay healthy was the hound, Jupe. He had developed a trick that kept him supplied with meat.

Dave followed him one day when he strayed off from the train. Jupe trotted purposefully up a rocky draw and disappeared. When Dave reached the top of the butte, he saw the hound crawling on his belly toward a slope that was dotted with sunning prairie dogs. They stood erect by their burrows or scurried about, visiting one another. Jupe kept himself hidden by clumps of sage till he was within ten or twelve yards, then made a sudden dash that took him into the midst of the colony. A snap of his big jaws, and he had one of the plump creatures before it could dive into its hole.

Their painful progress took the movers past Courthouse Rock, then Chimney Rock, and on toward Scotts Bluffs, where the naked cliffs stood high above the river.

Jeff Barlow didn't do much painting in those days. His scouting took him far ahead, and often he was away overnight. But when he returned, he nearly always brought fresh meat—deer or elk or antelope—and he helped cheer up the tired emigrants.

"One more day," he told them, "and we'll reach Horse Creek. There's pretty good grass there, an' clear water. Might be a good idea to rest there a bit—let the critters graze an' the ladies do some o' their laundry."

The exchange of visits with Running Wolf and the Crows had been of some value. It had helped most of the movers change their ideas about Indians. There were some, however, who couldn't forget the massacre of the small New Orleans train, and they still worried over the possibility that some band of savages might return to murder them. Dave asked Jeff about it when they were resting at Horse Creek.

"I reckon that particular bunch is long gone," he said. "Running Wolf told me they were Ogallala Sioux, just as I thought. But they were way out o' their own country, an' after they had a scuffle with the Crow party, they high-tailed it back east. We might see a Cheyenne or two, but they won't be troublesome this close to Fort Laramie."

The animals had gained a little strength, and the spirits of the people were higher when the train moved northwest once more. By making a long day of it, they were within sight of the cottonwoods on Laramie Creek at sundown. All agreed that they should push ahead to the stream before stopping. So it was that darkness had fallen before they made camp for the night.

Dave crawled out of his blanket at daybreak and went down to the creek to wash. It was when he lifted his dripping head from the water that he had his first sight of Fort Laramie. It stood less than half a mile away on the farther side of the stream, and the slant rays of the early sun were just catching the high white clay walls. From where he was, the fort looked like a palace of shining marble.

They made their crossing that morning, the cattle and horses swimming and wading, while the wagons rode the bottom, floor-deep. Luckily, it had been dry for the past week, so the creek was lower than usual. Nothing of any value was lost or damaged by water.

Just as the last wagon struggled up the bank, a crash of thunder came rolling down from the hills. The sky, Dave realized, had grown dark while they were making the crossing, and now black clouds, shot with streaks of lightning, hung over the valley.

"Quick!" Jeff Barlow shouted. "Get the children under cover!"

The mothers shooed their little ones into the wagons and climbed in after them. And within seconds the rain came down in such torrents as Dave had rarely seen.

He crawled under the wagon for some protection, while his father and the other men grabbed ponchos or slickers and sloshed about, quieting the uneasy horses and cattle. On the other side of the Laramie, another wagon train, larger than theirs, had come up behind them, ready to cross the ford. But within minutes the water had risen so high and was rushing down so fast that the new movers had to huddle under the canvas covers and wait the storm out.

For an hour the awesome thunder and lightning and the drenching rain continued. Then suddenly the roar subsided. The sun came out, shining on the wet hides of the cattle and the sodden wagon tops.

"Well," said Barlow cheerfully, "it washed some o' the trail dust off us, anyhow."

Dave crawled out from beneath the wagon. "Gosh!" he said. "Does it always rain that hard out here?"

"It's June," Jeff told him. "Got to expect a few cloudbursts this time o' year. We've been lucky up to now."

"What about those folks over yonder?" Dave asked. "How long do you figure they'll have to wait?"

Jeff looked at the river. "Not more'n a day," he guessed, "unless it comes on to rain again. It's just as well for us, though. If too many wagons an' people come in all at once, things get a bit crowded here at the fort."

Dave looked again at the structure he had admired that morning. The view was considerably less romantic now, for the adobe walls were wet and mottled with gray. He could also see a scattering of huts near the gate and dejected-looking Indians in blankets, who wandered slowly from one hovel to the next.

Jeff followed his gaze. "Trading-post Injuns," he commented with scorn. "They used to hunt buffalo an' trap fur. Now all they do is hang around here, hoping for a chance to beg or steal the price of a drink o' whisky."

"What tribe are they?" Dave asked.

"Who knows? Sioux, Cheyenne, Paiute—all proud tribes until they get a taste for liquor. Then they turn into animals, like these."

Mrs. March and the other women climbed down from their wagons, glad to sniff the fresh air after being cooped up inside. Some, Dave saw, had put on their best bonnets, eager to visit the fort and do some shopping.

Jeff looked at them and shook his head. "Reckon they're going to be sort o' disappointed," he said. "Fort Laramie's a long way from being another St. Louis!"

Seven

Dave's mother looked him over critically. "Finish your soup," she said, "an' get spruced up 'fore you go over to the fort."

She went to the wagon and came back with a pair of scissors. "One thing you need," she told him, "is a haircut. The way it hangs over your eyes an' down your neck, you look like an Injun. Pretty near as brown, too, the way the sun's burned you."

With vigorous strokes she snipped off the offending hair, then stood back and looked him over. "Not like a barber'd cut it," she said, "but this'll have to do. Now give me that dirty shirt an' get into a fresh one."

Half an hour later, wearing decently clean clothes and with his hair slicked down, Dave went with some of the other boys to visit the fort. As they neared the gate, Sol Jenkins looked about him with a puzzled frown. "I don't see no soldiers," he remarked. "No cannon, neither. You reckon we have to give the password to git in?"

The others couldn't answer, so they moved on, slowly and diffidently. The gate was made of heavy logs, but it stood wide open, hanging on a broken hinge. The quadrangle inside was cluttered with trash, and the only living things they saw were two mongrel dogs and a drunken Indian, all asleep in the sun. Opposite the gate was a door leading into the trading post, and toward this they walked.

Inside, they found themselves in a big, dimly lighted room. A few men from the train were there, looking over the stock of goods. The trader himself was a fat, swarthy French Canadian, who stood behind the dirty counter, haggling with two Indian trappers. For their furs each got a length of sleazy red calico, a plug of tobacco, and a bottle of cheap whisky. These seemed to comprise most of the store's stock in trade. For the people of the wagon trains, however, the proprietor kept a few dingy boxes of sewing materials, ribbons, buttons, and the like. And back of the counter he had a good supply of gunpowder and lead.

Rickety stairs led upward to a gallery, which opened onto cubicles where trappers and other visitors could sleep. The boys could see two or three such men up there, drinking and playing cards.

"Gosh!" Sol Jenkins murmured in disgust. "Some fort!"

There was nothing there to interest Dave and his friends, and they went back to the train greatly disillusioned.

Jeff Barlow met them with a grin. "I reckon you think," he said, "that an Injun war party could wipe Fort Laramie off the map. Well, it's been tried once or twice. But there's usually enough old sure-shot mountain men around to discourage 'em. Besides, the Injuns like to have a place to trade. Guess I'll trot over there myself an' see if I know anybody."

Thomas March had brought out the forge and was hard at work shoeing stock and mending wagons. "You, Dave," he called, "get out there an' keep a good eye on the cattle. Your ma can pump the bellows."

Guarding the cattle wasn't easy, for most of the grass had been eaten off near the fort, and the animals tended to stray away in search of food. It took all the boys and some of the men to keep them from wandering out of sight. Since the pasture was bounded on one side by the river and on another by a steep hillside, the main effort of the guards was to keep the cows and horses away from the ragged tepees and mud huts where the Indians lived.

Dave had gone over to the rocky rise at the foot of the butte, to drive back one of the oxen when suddenly he heard a sharp whirring sound. Looking down in alarm, he saw a coiled rattlesnake within a yard of his leg. Just as he jumped, the wicked head darted forward, and the fangs struck the heel of his cowhide boot.

Shaken and scared, Dave ran off a few steps, then turned and picked up a rock twice the size of his fist. His aim was good. The rock crushed the rattler's head, and though it still writhed violently, he knew it was as good as dead.

It was hot there in the sun. Dave looked around him, and to his horror he saw another snake, even larger, lying on a warm ledge a little higher up. This one had given no warning as yet. He armed himself with more stones, climbed to a point where he was above the big diamond-back, and killed it as he had the first. Proudly he carried the two heavy bodies back to camp.

"What have you got there, boy?" his mother called. "Rattlers, eh? Well, don't bring 'em any closer. You never can tell when a snake's dead."

"That's right, Dave," his father told him sternly. "Get 'em out o' here an' throw 'em away."

Unhappily, Dave carried his prizes back toward the butte. At least he could cut off the rattles and save them as keepsakes.

The larger snake had fifteen rattles, the smaller one twelve. With his knife he hacked off the trophies and left the bodies for the coyotes and buzzards.

He showed the tails to Jeff Barlow when the scout returned from the fort.

"I reckon you were lucky," Jeff said. "There were likely a dozen more snakes all around you in the rocks. They den up there, an' it's a good place to keep away from when the hot sun brings 'em out."

There was another heavy thundershower that night. The downpour caught Dave asleep under the wagon, and before he could get his poncho around him, he was wet to the skin. At daybreak he was up and trying to find dry wood to build a fire. Fortunately, the exercise stopped his shivering, and once the sun came up, his clothes were soon dry.

The added rain had swelled the creek still higher, so that the large train was still stuck on the other side. A few men swam their horses over and visited the fort, then stopped to chat with Doane and the others. They said they had started from Independence two days behind and made up the time on the trail. Since they were traveling without a blacksmith, they were anxious to have Dave's father shoe some of their horses. They had seen no buffalo and no Indians since leaving the Kaw. In fact, it sounded to Dave as if they must have had a pretty dull journey.

In the middle of the afternoon, Mrs. March and two or three other women put on their Sunday clothes and marched over to Fort Laramie. They were bent on making some purchases and thought this might be their last chance.

Dave's mother was fuming when she came back to the wagon. "Never saw such a measly lot o' merchandise," she snorted. "Nothing there fit for anybody but Injuns. Imagine

—no ribbons—an' the only needles he had were rusty! Besides that, there was enough dirt an' dust around to plant a cabbage patch!"

* * *

The train cut its stop at Fort Laramie to three days. The grazing was too poor to help the animals, and once the big group of wagons crossed, the space near the fort was overcrowded. Also it was now nearing the end of June. To reach the Columbia River within the next three months was the hope of every mover in the party.

Dave yoked up the four-ox team and cracked his bullwhip over their bony backs. All along the line the wagons were creaking into motion.

"Dad," the boy called, as his father rode near, "how far do you figure we've come since Independence?"

"Better'n six hundred miles, I reckon."

"An' how much farther do we have to go to get to the Willamette?"

"They tell me thirteen hundred miles—an' worse going than anything yet. We've got more'n two-thirds o' the trip still ahead of us. But we'll make it. The critters are a lot tougher'n they were when we started—an' so are the people."

The trail led on, northwestward. First it clung to the lower slopes along the Platte. Then, where the river made a bend, it cut over rocky foothills and across dry gulches. Off to the left was a real mountain, high and rugged, that Jeff Barlow said was Laramie Peak. It was only visible when the wagons were on top of a ridge. Most of the time they seemed to be in the canyon bottoms or toiling up hills so steep that all the passengers got out and walked.

It was the downhill grades that worried them most. No brakes could hold the heavier wagons on some of the pitches, and it was necessary to tie ropes to the rear axle and let the vehicles down by hand, with half the men in the train hanging on.

Then would come the climb up the opposite side. It usually took double-teaming, with as many as eight oxen hauling a wagon and men heaving at each wheel. By the time they reached the top, both the movers and the cattle were almost too weary to stand up. It was rough on the women and small children, too, for in order to lighten the wagons, everyone had to go up and down the hills on foot.

Dave didn't mind these hardships as much as he did the alkali dust that powdered all their clothing and got into their eyes and noses. In the fierce heat of noonday, it was all the drivers could do to keep the teams from heading toward water that had collected in white-rimmed sinkholes along the trail. Jeff Barlow went ahead and planted sticks with red rags to mark such places.

"One quick drink o' that stuff'd knock out a horse or a steer," he warned, "let alone a man."

A few streams flowed down from the hills, and whenever they came to one, they made camp, for sometimes two or three days would pass without their finding any good water. One such spot that stayed in their memories was Deer Creek.

It was the kind of stopping place Dave had dreamed about. The water was fresh and clear, and it came brawling down over the stones or eddying into deep pools where trout were jumping. There was good grass to pasture the stock, and a broad fringe of trees provided plenty of firewood. Best of all, Jeff Barlow thought there might be some hunting farther up the stream.

It made Dave happy when the guide asked him to come along, and he hurried to get his rifle, bullet pouch, and powder horn. Together the pair rode up the creek. At times they had to wade their horses when the stream was shut in by the canyon walls. After three or four miles, the valley widened into a wooded glade, and Jeff decided they should dismount and tie the horses. Warning Dave to be silent, he led the way forward, his moccasins making no sound in the mossy undergrowth.

They held their guns ready and advanced cautiously, eyes scanning the thickets and trees ahead.

"Hold it, boy!" Jeff whispered as he held up a warning hand. "There's grass up yonder, an' I see something grazing—big buck deer, maybe."

The wind was blowing down the valley toward the hunters. They bent low and kept their bodies hidden behind the screening bushes as they crept forward. When they had been moving in this way for several minutes, the outline of the animal could be seen more clearly. To Dave it looked as big as a horse. He might have taken it for one except for the huge rack of antlers on its lowered head.

"Elk!" Jeff breathed.

They crawled on another twenty yards before they were within range. Then the scout motioned to Dave to take the shot. "Low down—behind the shoulder," he whispered. "Keep cool an' steady."

It was easier to say than to do. Dave drew a long breath, waiting for the shaky feeling to leave him. Then he slowly raised his rifle and took aim. With the pressure of his finger on the trigger came the crashing report, and he saw the elk give a mighty bound.

"You hit him!" Barlow cried. "Come on!"

By the time they emerged from the woods, the big animal had fallen and was thrashing about on the ground. Jeff rushed in with his hunting knife and mercifully finished the job.

"Nice bull," he commented. "Horns are in velvet this time

o' year. See how thick an' soft they look? But he's a fine big one. Run maybe eight hundred pounds, so we'll need the horses to carry all the meat. Suppose you go fetch 'em while I start to work on the critter."

Dave hurried back and led the two ponies up through the woods. When the smell of blood reached them, they snorted and reared, but he held onto their reins, and with soothing words he managed to bring them within forty feet. They would approach no nearer, so he tied them there.

"Never could figure it out." Jeff chuckled. "That horse o' mine isn't a mite spooked by a dead buffalo, but he's scared to death when he smells elk."

They wrapped the meat in two big bundles of skin, and after Jeff had calmed the horses, these were tied on behind their saddles. Then the hunters mounted and rode triumphantly back to the wagons.

There was rejoicing in the camp that night, for not only did they dine royally on elk venison, but there were also fine big trout as well. Some of the men and boys had spent the afternoon fishing.

When the meal was finished, Thomas March stretched himself and grinned. "If the trip to Oregon was all like this," he said, "it'd be a reg'lar picnic, wouldn't it?"

Jeff Barlow happened by in time to hear the remark and shook his head. "Better eat hearty, folks," he said, "an' get a good night's sleep. In a couple more days we'll cross the Platte an' head up the Sweetwater into the high country. There'll be no more picnics—just hard pulling an' short feed, all the way to the Pass."

"That's all right," the blacksmith answered stoutly. "I reckon we can take it."

Eight

The wagons lined out with shouts and a cracking of whips, and Dave fell in behind the loose stock that brought up the rear. It was a sultry morning, with no breeze and a blazing sun.

By noon, when they rested after a dozen miles, the sky was black in the west. Doane hurried up the movers, anxious to get on the trail again before the rain came. Soon they were plodding forward once more, eyes on the cloudbank and ears tuned to catch the muttering of far-off thunder. The cattle lowed nervously and shook their horns.

After a few miles, Dave rode to the wagon to get his slicker. All along the train he could hear children crying and mothers speaking to them crossly. The ominous weather had brought a tension that was felt by all.

It was nearing four o'clock when the storm hit them. The wagons circled hastily into the shelter of a cliff, and the covers were snugged tight. The wind howled down out of the hills, driving the rain in solid sheets, and the crash of thunder was like artillery. Drenched and frightened, the animals turned their rumps to the deluge and stood trembling with heads hung down.

Dave was sure they were too wet and miserable to run away. He tied Cinder to a wheel of the March wagon and crawled in under the flap at the rear. The little girls were cowering in a dark corner, and his father and mother sat on trunks near the entrance.

"Come on in, son," said Sarah March. "Take off your slicker an' sit down. You can't get things any wetter'n they already are."

Gratefully, he joined them and pulled the flap to behind him. "Seems as if everything's bigger out here," he grumbled. "Rivers an' mountains an' thunderstorms—they all come outsized!"

The storm lasted a good hour, then ended with surprising suddenness. The wind dropped to nothing, the rain ceased, and a dripping silence fell over the wagons. When Dave stepped outside, the westering sun shone brilliantly over the edge of the butte, glinting on the wet canvas. People began to hail each other cheerfully, like the survivors of a flood.

After consulting with Jeff Barlow, Doane decided the train should move on before camping for the night. The oxen were yoked again, the loose stock rounded up, and they made another three or four miles before their final halt.

The next day was practically a repetition of that one. Heat, followed by darkening skies, ended in another violent shower. But before sunset they had reached the crossing of the Platte. Dave rode down to the riverbank and stared at the foaming, muddy water. There he was joined by Jeff Barlow.

"Doesn't look passable, does it?" said the scout. "Well, we'll just have to wait till morning and see. She may go down a couple o' feet by then."

The wagon owners spent a bad night worrying about the crossing. Before breakfast they gathered on the bank to watch Barlow try the ford on horseback. Halfway over, the pinto was forced to swim, and the current carried him fifty yards downstream before he found footing on the other side. After a brief rest for the pinto, he rode along the bank and swam back.

"She's still a bit too deep," he told them calmly. "Getting lower, though. If it doesn't rain again, we can cross this afternoon. One thing I'd do is get together some driftwood logs while you're waiting. You'll be pretty sure to need 'em to float your wagons."

He opened the waterproof pack strapped to his mule's saddle and pulled out a big drawing pad and some charcoal pencils. In a moment he was seated on a stump, sketching the lively scene around him.

Dave took an ax and went with a party of men and boys to round up some logs. There were masses of dead trees and limbs piled up along the riverbank by past floods. They chopped them into handy lengths and brought teams of oxen to drag them to the waiting train. Then began the job of lashing the logs to the sides of each wagon. Fortunately, all the movers had coils of rope as part of their equipment.

Now the oxen were rested, the noon meal was cooked and eaten, and all that remained was to wait for the level of water in the river to go down. Dave stood on the bank and watched the measuring stick he had driven into the mud. Inch by inch, more of it was now visible above the current, but he knew the water was still too deep.

Off to the northeast, on the farther side of the Platte, rose the steep rusty-colored cliffs of the Red Buttes. Now, in the midday heat, their tops seemed to shimmer against the sky, and he saw them as another symbol of the vast, impersonal bigness of this savage land.

Two hours passed, and the west began to darken once more. The men and women watched the gathering clouds anxiously. Then Barlow rose, put away his sketches, and went down to the bank.

"All right, folks," he announced. "I think we can make it now. You'll be carried downstream a way, but no harm in that. An' if we wait till it rains again, you'll never get across."

He mounted his pinto, took a double hitch on the mule's halter, and rode into the river. Behind him, Doane whipped up his reluctant horses, and the other wagons followed, one by one. Dave rode on the upstream side of the lead oxen, urging them on as the water grew deeper. Star's eyes rolled in terror, and he gave a plaintive bellow before starting to swim. Then the whole train was breasting the current, the wagons leaning crazily under the push of the river. At last Cinder was able to touch bottom, and a minute later the oxen, too, had found solid footing.

"I'll keep 'em going," Thomas March called from the driver's seat. "You go back an' help with the loose stock, boy."

Dave let the pony breathe for a moment, then turned her to swim back the way they had come. As he did so, there came a yell from the middle of the river, and he saw the Skellys' wagon, the last in line, go over on its side. It was a rickety vehicle to start with and had probably been badly loaded. But there were children aboard, and Dave kicked Cinder's ribs to make her swim to the collapsed wagon as fast as possible.

Mrs. Skelly's screams told him he was too late. A dozen yards below, a small, tousled head bobbed in the current and went under. With rein and knee, Dave guided the black mare past the floundering oxen, aiming for the spot where the child had last appeared. For a frantic instant he strained forward, finding nothing. Then the little white face rose to the surface again, and leaning out from the saddle, he was able to seize the child by her calico dress. He dragged the limp little body across his saddle bow and turned for the north bank once more.

Others had seen the catastrophe and were on their way to the wagon, but Dave knew the small girl needed more help than they could give her there. As soon as the pony scrambled out, Jeff Barlow was there to meet them.

"Give her to me," he said. "She's mighty near drowned."

Gently, he laid the little girl on her stomach and pushed down with his hands against her ribs, then released the pressure. Water streamed from her mouth, and she gave a strangled gasp. Again and again he repeated the action till at last she was breathing almost normally.

"There," he said. "She'll live—mostly thanks to you."

Dave shook his head. "I thought she was gone," he choked. "But I've got to get back to the herd."

Cinder seemed to think she had done enough swimming, but at his stern command she breasted the current once again. On the south bank the cattle were milling about in confusion while the herdsmen tried to force them into the water. It took half an hour to get them rounded up and headed in the right direction. A peal of thunder over the western mountains helped frighten them into swimming, and by the time the rain started, nearly all the animals were safely over. The only losses from the crossing of the Platte were one sickly calf and some worthless pieces of furniture from the capsized wagon.

That night, after the shower had passed and the people of the train were gathered around their supper fires, Dave found himself being hailed as a hero. Skelly was still angry over the mishap to his wagon, but his scrawny little wife came to thank Dave for saving her daughter. She broke into tears and had to be comforted by Mrs. March. After she had gone, the blacksmith's wife turned to her son.

"What you did was right," she said sternly, "but it's only what any decent person would do. So don't get any biggety ideas. Come on—wash up an' eat."

* * *

Several of the men pitched in to help repair the broken wagon, and the next morning the train was ready to move again. The trail led overland to the Sweetwater, which flowed into the Platte some thirty miles upriver from the place where they had crossed. That night they had to make a dry camp, but their water barrels had been filled before they left the river. It was the first day of July.

"We're still right on schedule," Jeff Barlow remarked to Dave as he rode back along the train and passed the March wagon. "Two days or three, an' we'll get to Independence Rock. That's what the early movers called it because they reached there on July 4—Independence Day. The Sweetwater's got a lot o' landmarks where things have happened, like Injun massacres an' families being wiped out by sickness. It's a rough trip, but there's no other way to get to the South Pass."

When they stopped for their nooning, Dave wandered ahead up the trail. There he found one of the markers his friend had mentioned. Five stones were piled up, topped by an ox skull, and a wooden slat was thrust between the stones. On the board were words rudely cut with a knife. "Mary Grover," he read. "Bit by a Snake, 6 July, 1841. Aged 5 Yrs."

Even as he stood there, a big rattler crawled out of a hole in the rocks and coiled itself in the sun. Dave didn't bother to kill it. There were probably a hundred more hidden in the stony crevices within fifty yards of where he stood. He went back to the train and warned the movers to keep their children close to the wagons.

The heat that day was nearly unbearable. The great bowl of the sky above them was white-hot, reflecting the sun's rays like a burning glass, and both men and animals faltered under it as they struggled on. Dave's father was grim-faced as he lashed the long-suffering oxen.

"Reckon it hurts me more'n it does them to drive 'em so," he growled through parched lips. "But it's got to be done if we're to make Oregon."

Relief came at last with the end of the day. The sun set

early behind high mountains to the west, and even before it disappeared, the air was noticeably cooler. Within an hour the evening had grown chilly, though the rocks held the heat most of the night.

It was the morning of the third day since the Platte crossing when they sighted the Sweetwater. Here was a wholly different kind of river. Instead of being wide and muddy and laced with sandbars, this stream was deep and fast-running. It came tumbling down through a gorge, then spread into a calmer pool, where Jeff Barlow said it was possible to cross.

The train camped near the ford, for there was good grass and shade and a chance for the women to wash clothes in clear water. Dave and two or three of the men rode their horses over to the farther bank, finding firm bottom all the way. A mile or two upstream to the westward loomed a towering pinnacle of stone, and Dave galloped his pony toward it, sure in his own mind what it was.

When he pulled up by the base of the rock, he could see a dozen inscriptions cut into the soft stone. As he had expected, the lowest and largest one announced that this was Independence Rock. It bore the date of July 4, 1839, and beneath it were the names of several men—perhaps members of one of the earliest wagon trains.

Others who had followed after had carved their names or initials higher, and a few daring ones must have climbed a hundred feet or more up the sheer face of the cliff. Dave was tempted to try it himself, but before he could dismount, he heard a hail behind him.

"I'm going on a hunt," called Jeff Barlow. "Want to come along?"

"Sure," Dave replied, "but I haven't got my rifle."

"Never mind. We probably won't find much to shoot at, anyhow."

They rode on along the narrow path between the cliff and the river. A little way beyond, the valley widened again, giving room for a patch of scraggly woods, too thin to provide much cover.

"No deer in here," Jeff commented. "We'll run into more game when we get higher up in the mountains, but that'll take another week, an' the camp needs meat right now."

Beyond the trees they came to a little trickle of water that angled down from the hills, and Jeff led the way up the narrow bed of the rivulet. They rode for two or three miles without seeing a tree or any living thing. Then the canyon became broader and shallower. A few pines grew out of the rocky soil, and in the distance they could see the higher mountain slopes covered with dark forest.

Suddenly, Cinder snorted and shied, and right at her feet Dave saw a squat grayish-brown animal waddling toward a hole in the bank. It had a long snout, and its teeth were bared in a surly snarl.

"Badger," said Jeff with a chuckle. "If you've never seen one before, they're mean-looking customers. But they're too slow to do any damage to a horse."

At the lower edge of the pines, he dismounted and handed the pinto's bridle rein to Dave. "You stay here," he said, "an' keep the horses quiet. I'll go in an' see what I can stir up."

The boy felt frustrated but did as he was told. He vowed to himself that he would never go on another scouting expedition without his gun. He saw Jeff vanish into the thick growth and sat there waiting while the ponies foraged for grass.

Minutes dragged on into half an hour, and he heard no report from Jeff's rifle. Deep in the woods, a distant crow cawed its warning, so he figured that must be about where the scout was. Once a mother coyote and two cubs came stealing out of the forest. They caught the horse scent and disappeared again so quickly that he had to rub his eyes to be sure he had seen them. More time passed. Then suddenly the pinto pricked up its ears, snorted, and jerked on the rein. Less than fifty yards from where he sat, Dave saw a huge animal come ambling into the open. It was the biggest bear he had ever seen or imagined.

The great beast showed no concern over their presence. Deliberately, it rose on its hind legs, sniffing the air with its lifted snout. It looked at least eight feet tall. Its belly was brownish and its back a pale silver gray that seemed to be almost white. He knew he must be looking at his first silver-tip grizzly—the giant that the mountain men called a "white bear."

Nine

The horses were terrified. It was all Dave could do to hang onto the reins and keep them from bolting while he watched the big bear. He was frightened himself but determined not to show it.

After what seemed a long time, the animal dropped to all fours once more and moved off southward along the edge of the woods. Dave drew a long breath of relief, patted Cinder's sweating neck, and spoke soothing words in an effort to calm the two ponies.

Hardly had the grizzly vanished beyond a ridge when Jeff came out of the forest. He carried the unused rifle in the crook of his arm and whistled a little tune as he approached.

"What spooked the horses?" he asked, noticing the pinto's rolling eyes.

"Oh, not much," Dave replied. "Just the biggest white bear you ever saw. He stood right up yonder and looked us over."

Jeff nodded. "Thought I saw some sign," he commented. "Well, the old fellow must have chased away all the game. We'd better get back to the train an' make sure the stock's kept in close tonight."

By midafternoon, the wagon owners decided it was time to ford the river. Even the women were ready to move. Their washing had dried, and they had rested for a while in the shade. It was nearly sunset when the last wagon had crossed. Then the loose stock was herded over and a fresh camp made on the south bank. After listening to Barlow's warning, Doane appointed six men to guard the cattle. Dave wanted to join them when he had eaten supper. He carefully loaded his rifle with an extra-heavy charge of powder and made certain his priming was fresh. If he saw that bear again, he wanted to be ready for him. However, his father overruled the idea, at least for the first part of the night.

"You'll get your chance later on," he said. "I'll take the first watch while you catch some sleep, an' I'll wake you up after a spell."

Despite his disappointment, Dave was tired enough to fall asleep at once. He woke about two o'clock in the morning with a big hand shaking him by the shoulder.

"Come on," his father whispered, "it's your turn now. So far all's quiet, an' I doubt if anything's likely to happen before dawn. Think you can keep awake?"

"O' course I can!" Dave told him. He picked up his rifle and went stumbling off in the darkness. By the time his eyes were able to pick out the shapes of things, there came a patter of feet behind him, and old Jupe thrust a cold nose against his hand.

The herd of cattle and horses had been driven in close to camp, and a couple of fires burned beyond the bedded animals. Several men and boys were sitting around the fires, feeding the flames occasionally with scraps of driftwood, and Dave took his place among them.

"Hi," growled Sol Jenkins in surly tones. "What's been

keepin' you? You ain't scairt, are you? I think the whole thing is foolishness, anyhow. Back home we've got bears, an' they'd run if you say 'Boo!' "

"Black bears? Sure," Dave replied. "I've seen 'em, too. But this one's three times as big and ten times as dangerous. Wait till *you* meet up with a grizzly!"

A breeze blowing down out of the mountains made the night cold. The watchers huddled close around the fire, and more than one fell asleep. It was after three o'clock in the morning when Dave felt Jupe stir beside him. The big hound scrambled to his feet, and there was a low rumble in his throat as he sniffed the air.

"What is it, boy?" Dave whispered. He threw another stick on the fire and checked the priming of his rifle. When the dog's growling grew louder, he stood up and stared out into the night.

Just then another noise roused the rest of the guards. It was a short, muffled animal sound, half moan, half scream, and it came from the direction of the cattle herd.

"Come on!" yelled Dave and started that way at a run, with Jupe galloping in front of him.

Someone from the other fire got there first. He was waving a blazing torch, and by its light Dave saw the huddled, milling cattle. One steer lay stretched on the ground and rearing above it, gigantic in the torchlight, stood the pale bulk of the bear.

Dave's hands shook, but he lifted his rifle and aimed at the brute's heart. He knew, even as he pulled the trigger, that he had fired too fast. The grizzly gave a squealing roar of pain and started to charge, not at him but at the man with the torch. It was Jeff Barlow, Dave saw now. The scout hurled the burning stick straight into the great beast's face, sidestepped, and raised his rifle, all in one fluid motion.

Meanwhile, the old hound had gone into action. Snapping and snarling, he sprang at the grizzly's flank, and though Dave tried desperately to call him back, he paid no heed. The bear whirled to smash this new tormentor, and at that instant Jeff's rifle shot rang out. With a grunt of surprise, the giant bear slumped to the ground in a furry heap, a bullet through its heart.

The cattle were still bellowing with fright, and it took time to settle them down once more. The young steer killed by the grizzly had been one of a pair that the Frosts were training to the yoke. It lay with its neck broken by one blow of the heavy paw.

"Gosh," said Sol Jenkins, staring at it. "I guess I spoke too quick about bears not amountin' to much!"

Jeff Barlow was examining the dead brute. "Your shot went a mite high an' got him in the neck," he told Dave. "Just hurt him enough to make him real dangerous. It would have been a mighty close thing for me if that old dog o' yours hadn't pitched in. When the bear turned on him, it gave me a clear shot."

Jupe came limping to his master's side, and Dave saw blood on his shoulder, where the great claws had raked him.

"Come on, old boy," he said. "Let's get back to the wagon so I can put something on that."

He found a can of salve in the catchall box at the tail of the wagon, and after washing the wound to get out the dirt, he smeared the ointment into the raw claw cuts. The old hound stood the pain without flinching, trusting Dave to take care of him.

The next morning Mr. Frost cut up the meat from his dead steer and shared it among the wagon families. He took the loss more calmly than Dave expected.

"Critter was too young to be much of any use yet," he said. "An' if I have to, I can always yoke the other steer with one o' my cows. Anyhow, Barlow's promised me the bearskin, so at least we'll have a warm rug for our cabin!"

* * *

It was a tired bunch of men that urged the oxen up the trail that July day. They moved slowly through the black jaws of the Devil's Gate before camping for the night. The day after, the train crawled on into another narrow canyon at a place called Split Rock, and the climbing grew steeper with every mile.

Sarah March, clumping along beside the wagon in her man's boots, mopped her forehead and pushed back a damp tendril of hair.

"How soon you reckon we'll rest, Dave?" she asked. "This heat an' the thin air up here makes me dizzy an' short o' breath."

"Whoa-up!" Dave called to the oxen. "You'd better ride a spell, Ma," he told her. "We're past the steepest part, an' they'll pull it easy whether you're in the wagon or not."

She hoisted her big body up over the front wheel and slumped, panting, on the driver's seat. "Be all right soon's I've had a bit o' rest," she said.

It wasn't like his mother to give in to discomfort, and Dave was worried about her. By the time they reached the next steep climb, she was on her feet again, trudging along as usual beside the wagon. But her son kept an anxious eye on her. When Thomas March rode up to take over the driving, Dave told him what had happened.

"I reckon it's the altitude," the blacksmith answered. "Your ma isn't used to it, an' that sun is mighty hot, besides. Don't fret, now. I'll see to it she rides more an' walks less."

The high, thin air hadn't given Dave any noticeable trouble, but he heard others complain. Most of the people in the train were lowlanders—farmers and merchants who had never been more than a thousand feet above sea level. Now, as Jeff Barlow estimated, they were in mile-high country, and it would be even higher by the time they reached the Continental Divide.

The stock, strangely enough, seemed to thrive in the high atmosphere. The horses and oxen were gaunt from hard work and short rations, but they now had plenty of water. Not an animal had dropped out yet, though the Skellys' and Pecks' teams looked like skin and bones.

Four days beyond Split Rock, the Sweetwater had to be forded once more. There were markers to show that the trail could no longer follow the south bank, and an arrow chiseled in the rock pointed the way to the best crossing. The water was low, and Jeff rode across first, his pony keeping its feet all the way. Since it was then only a little past noon, the men decided to go over at once. They made it without any accidents, and within less than an hour, the loose stock was also safely across. There the train camped, and the water barrels were refilled.

Jeff had scouted a bit farther up the trail. Now he came back to the March wagon.

"Want to let Dave come with me?" he asked the smith. "I found some sign o' game up yonder."

"Sure," said Thomas March, proud to have his son chosen. "Hope you can get us some fresh meat."

The two hunters rode off with as little stir as possible. When they were out of earshot, Jeff told his companion that he had found fresh buffalo signs.

"I reckon it's just a small bunch," he said. "Didn't want to scare 'em off with too many men."

Some two miles up the Sweetwater, Jeff reined his pony in and pointed to tracks in the mud. "They must have come down here to drink," he said. "It was two or three hours ago, I figure, an' not more'n a dozen buffalo in all. That means they're likely to be young bulls. Up to a couple o' years old, the bulls run by themselves. All the cows an' calves stay in bigger herds that are guarded by the old bulls. But young bull beef is good enough eating—'most as tender as young cow."

He picked up the trail and followed it north, up the side of a steep hill. Dave's pony scrambled along in the tracks of the pinto, her hoofs dislodging pebbles that rattled down the slope. He was afraid the noise might scare the game, but Jeff rode on, paying no attention. At last they reached the crest of the butte and looked off across a stretch of dry, rolling prairie. Most of the tufts of buffalo grass near them had been eaten off short.

The scout dismounted and studied the ground for a moment. "Here's where they went," he said, "northwest."

They went on, watching the trail for another mile. Then Jeff stood high in the stirrups for a better view. "There they are," he said quietly. "Just beyond that rise yonder, maybe a quarter of a mile off."

Dave stretched upward till he, too, saw the dark humps. Settling back in the saddle, he checked his rifle and made ready to ride. But Jeff ordered otherwise.

"This time," he said, "we'll leave the horses here an' stalk 'em on foot. If we each get one, that's all the meat we can use."

He hitched his pony's bridle rein to a sagebrush clump, and Dave did the same. The first hundred yards were quickly covered. After that they had to crouch low, keeping hidden by the crest of the rise.

"Easy now," Jeff whispered. "They can't see much, but there's nothing wrong with their ears an' noses. There's a cross wind, so I doubt if they'll catch our scent. Have to go mighty quiet, though."

He crawled over the top of the ridge and peered cautiously at the feeding herd. When Dave followed his lead, he saw a huddle of black shapes about two hundred yards away and slowly moving nearer as the buffalo grazed.

"We'll wait here for 'em," Jeff said under his breath. "Don't shoot till I give you a sign."

Dave had learned patience. He lay on his stomach behind a hummock of grass and watched the young bulls draw nearer. Sometimes they seemed to be rooted where they stood. Then one would come on a step or two, and the others would follow when they were ready.

Half an hour passed, and the range shortened till Dave was sure he could hit his target. He saw Jeff move his rifle forward an inch at a time.

"I'll take the one to the left," the scout whispered. "You pick your own."

Together they pulled back their hammers, and at the double click the nearest buffalo raised his head. Dave aimed at the brisket below the bearded chin and squeezed the trigger gently. At the same instant Jeff fired, and two buffalo went down. The rest of the little herd turned and galloped off to the northward.

"Good shooting, boy," said Jeff laconically. "Suppose you go an' bring the horses while I start on the hides an' meat."

Within an hour the choicest rib steaks, hump meat, livers, and tongues were wrapped in the still-warm skins and tied on the ponies' rumps behind their saddles. Cinder and the pinto were both trained buffalo horses, and the smell of the blood didn't make them skittish.

The hunters rode back to camp just as the supper fires were being started, and the whole train feasted that night. Barlow strolled past the March wagon where Dave was gnawing on a juicy rib bone.

"Make the most of it," said the scout with a grin. "We aren't likely to find any more buffalo from now on."

Ten

Dave heard the distant howling of wolves that night and shivered as he thought of the hungry beasts tearing at the carcasses they had left on the mesa. The train pulled out early the next morning, and when the wagons reached the spot where the young bulls had come down to drink, he saw the dark shapes of buzzards circling in the sky, off to the north. Soon, he knew, the bones would be picked clean.

The going grew harder hour by hour, and the people walked beside their wagons as the oxen panted up the grades. The sun beat down fiercely on the travelers. Sunbonnets protected the women, but the men and the children were burned to a dark tan. An hour before sunset, the train halted on a fairly level spot, too worn out to go farther. They had, Doane estimated, covered fifteen miles that day, and Jeff told them two more such days would bring them to the South Pass.

The Continental Divide! Pacific Spring, where the water flowed west to the Pacific instead of east to the Gulf! It seemed to the tired travelers that if they could once reach that point in their journey, the rest of the way would be all downhill. The scout didn't tell them how wrong they were, but Dave saw him shake his head in pity when he thought nobody was watching.

The train struggled on through another long day, camping for the night beside a little stream that cascaded down from the north. Just as the fires were being lighted, three men came riding down the draw. Dave heard the dogs barking furiously and went to see what was happening.

The newcomers made a terrifying sight. They wore great rough beards and were dressed in old buckskins, black with dirt and grease. Two of them wore mangy fur caps. Each was mounted on a gaunt, shaggy pony and led an equally decrepit pack horse, carrying traps and bundles of furs. They would have ridden past, but Jeff Barlow let out a whoop and ran to greet them.

In a moment the strangers had dismounted and were embracing the young scout with shouts of laughter and queer-sounding words.

"Wal, hoss!" one cried. "Heap long time no see! How floats yore stick?"

Jeff invited the trio to share his own campfire, and after supper he introduced them.

"Time you folks met some real mountain men," he said. "This here's Zeke Boyle, an' this un's Shorty MacNair. Then the hard-looking feller with the big stomach is my old trapping pardner, Pete LeBlanc. They're on their way across to the Green River rendezvous, bringing out their skins to sell to the traders."

Pete LeBlanc was a jolly-faced Frenchman, fat but powerfully built. "She's awful poor season," he remarked. "Beaver, she don' come in de traps no more."

"That's right," MacNair grumbled. "Not more'n half as many plew as we used to take out, an' the price is down, too."

Zeke Boyle chuckled through his ragged beard. "Don't worry, boys," he said. "We got enough fer one big spree when we git to the Green, anyhow. Me—I aim to stay drunk fer a week!"

"Where'd you winter?" Jeff asked. "Did you find that valley where we got so much fur, Pete?"

The Frenchman shook his head. "No good dere no more," he replied. "All trap' out."

"We was over on one o' the streams that feed into Beaver Creek," MacNair put in. "Reckon they'll have to change the name to No-Beaver Creek 'less'n the critters come back there."

"Did you run into any Indians?" Doane inquired.

"Seen some Blackfoot sign," Boyle said. "That was back in the fall, though, an' they don't often git this fur south. Why—you folks had any Injun trouble?"

"No," Jeff replied. "An' don't want any."

"You still paint de pictures?" LeBlanc asked him with a grin.

"That's right. I took this scout job partly so I could draw a wagon train firsthand. I'd better get a sketch o' you boys tomorrow, though—draw you before you have a chance to clean up an' get your hair cut!"

Long after Dave turned in, Jeff and the three mountain men were still laughing and telling stories around the fire. But they were all up by dawn. While the wagons were being loaded and the teams yoked up, the scout was making quick sketches of his old trapping companions. He caught the relaxed ease of their muscular bodies, along with the worn buckskins, beards, and straggly hair.

MacNair grinned at him. "Never thought to see an old winterer like you messin' with oxen," he remarked. "What's wrong with hosses?"

"Shows your ignorance," Jeff answered with a smile. "You

take a good ox an' he'll outpull an' outlast a horse every time. Better for a steep, narrow trail, too. An ox is near as sure-footed as a goat. Only one thing—a horse can move quicker. But he won't make many more miles in a day."

"All right!" said MacNair. "I'll believe you—only don't ask me to ride one o' the critters!"

The trappers rode in front of the train all that day, helping pull some of the wagons up the cruel grades as they neared the crest of the South Pass. They went up the final ascent a little before sundown and camped that night on the farther side.

The movers crowded together, standing openmouthed to stare at the vast stretch of country beyond. The mountains rolled away at their feet like waves of the sea, dark and forest-crowned, mile after mile, to dim snow-capped ranges on the far horizon. One of the women started to sing a hymn, "Praise God from Whom All Blessings Flow," and Sarah March joined in, her strong voice echoing among the cliffs. It was a solemn moment for that weary band.

After supper Jeff invited Dave to ride with him down the trail to the west. The trappers had already pushed on, anxious to reach the Green and slake their thirst with trade whisky.

It was dusk when Jeff pulled up his pinto by a heap of rocks alongside the trail. He dismounted and took off his hat as he stood looking at the pyramid of stones.

"I helped build this monument," he said quietly. "One o' my best friends is buried here—old Wind River Slim. He was mighty good to me. We were bringing in our beaver to the rendezvous when a bunch o' young Cheyenne bucks attacked us. Slim took an arrow through the lungs, an' nothing we did could save him."

Dave felt as sober as if he had been in church. He could see that Jeff was deeply moved by the memory of his old friend, and Dave kept silent, waiting till the moment was over.

* * *

Pacific Spring, when they reached it the next day, was somewhat disappointing. Dave had pictured a fine pool of gushing water. Instead, after much hunting they found a tiny trickle hidden under leaves and moss. It was impossible to trace it back to its source, but there was no question about the direction of the flow. A mile below, the rivulet had widened enough for them to fill their water barrels, a precaution that the scout urged them to take.

"We're following a short cut," he said, "over high land to the Upper Green. Here an' at the Big Sandy are about the only places we can be sure o' finding water. But it'll save us at least two days—maybe three."

It was a long day's haul across to the Big Sandy, and there they refilled the barrels, for much of their water had evaporated in the fierce midsummer heat. Then, though it was already sunset, Jeff Barlow recommended that they start rolling again.

"You aren't as tired as you think," he told the assembled men. "It's a forty-mile pull over to the Green and nothing much but hot sand, the first half of it. Traveling at night, you and the animals won't suffer so much, but I have to tell you it'll be a rough trip anyhow."

Some objected that their cattle were too tired, but the majority finally agreed to try it. They set out at dusk.

The country they traversed that night was like the surface of a burned-out planet—nothing but rocks and sand and empty craters, so parched that no blade of grass grew. Fortunately, the moon shed an eerie light that showed Jeff the way, for there was really no recognizable trail.

Dave plodded beside the panting oxen, so weary that he could barely keep his eyes open. There was no talk—only muttered grunts and curses when some mover stumbled over a stone or fell into a hole. The wheels creaked, and the wagons lurched, and the bumpy ride brought whimpers from the little children inside.

When at last the sky began to gray with approaching daylight, the train came to a stop. Water was rationed out to the thirsty animals, then a cup for each human, and the women started kettles boiling for coffee or tea. Most of the men slept for an hour or two in the shade of the wagons. Then Jeff urged them on once more.

"You can't stay here," he said. "There's no feed for the cattle, and they might as well be hauling as standing in the sun."

As the day grew hotter, the ground seemed to get even worse. There were sharp ridges to climb, and over and over again the men had to strain at the wheels, forcing the wagons upward. Dave looked at his father and saw his face drawn and gray with dust. He walked heavily, too, with none of the usual spring in his step. But his bleary eyes were set on the western horizon, and he pushed on without flinching.

There was no stop for a noon meal. In that blistering heat, nobody even thought of it. A short time later, two oxen dropped exhausted, then a horse and another ox. Their owners tried to revive them with precious water or whip them to their feet, but it was no use. They died where they lay, their sad eyes glazing, and more animals were brought from the loose herd to take their places.

The nightmare journey continued, hour after terrible hour, till men and beasts alike moved like sleepwalkers. Ahead of them the hot circle of the sun was finally cut in two by mountain peaks. And then, just as dusk was falling, Jeff galloped his gaunt pinto back to the head of the train.

"It's there!" he cried in a cracked voice. "Right close! We've made it to the Green!"

Some tried to cheer. Others simply goaded the tired oxen and staggered on. In a few minutes they topped a rise and looked down the shadowy slope toward trees and grass and flowing water. Never had a sight been more beautiful.

The men and the stock were all so travel-worn that no effort was made that night to picket the horses or guard the herd. As soon as they had drunk their fill and eaten a few mouthfuls of food, they simply fell down beside the wagons and slept.

Dave woke to the singing of birds and stared around him at the lovely green of foliage and the bright colors of flowers. He scrambled up, washed himself at the river, and went to gather wood for the morning fire. A little way downstream he saw Jeff and ran to meet him.

"Howdy," said the scout. "I just wanted to make sure none o' the stock had strayed. Look at 'em! To see 'em eat, you'd think they hadn't tasted grass in a month!"

That was a restful day in the green valley by the riverbank. The women and girls washed and dried clothes, while some of the boys went upstream to fish. The men made a show of repairing wagons and gear, but they stayed in the shade and did more talking than actual working. Jeff rode across the ford to the forest on the other side and came back at noon with a mule deer slung over his saddle.

"Plenty o' game in the woods 'round here," he remarked. "I reckon that means there aren't any Shoshonis close. We'd better keep our eyes peeled, though. I figure we were lucky last night not to have our horses stolen."

That evening when they were all relaxed and had eaten a good meal of venison, one of Doane's hired men produced a fiddle, and Mr. Jenkins brought out an old banjo from his wagon. For an hour or more, the people of the train sang. First came such old movers' favorites as "Sweet Betsy from Pike" and "Bound for the Promised Land." Then the tempo quickened, and the two musicians broke into "Turkey in the Straw." Soon laughing couples were on their feet, dancing as if the ordeal of the day before had never taken place. Dave was pleased to see his own parents join in a Virginia reel, the heat and the weary miles forgotten.

He caught a glimpse of Lucy Beeman's face across the ring of firelight, and she looked so wistful as she watched the whirling couples that he had an impulse to go over and ask her to dance. But he thought of the teasing the other boys would give him and sat there miserably, his heels beating out the lively rhythm. Then the music switched to "Skip to My Lou." Red-faced, Dave stood up and marched over to Lucy. "Lou" was the name she usually went by.

"Come on," he said gruffly. "Want to try it?"

She sprang to her feet, her eyes sparkling, and in a moment they were swinging with the older folks. That broke the ice. Several of the other youngsters paired off and joined the dancers.

Perhaps it was because of the harsh journey they had endured that all the members of the train felt a sense of release. In their joy they continued the harmless revelry till close to midnight, and nearly all of them slept till broad daylight the next morning. Only Jeff sat awake with his rifle and kept watch over the horses and cattle.

By common consent the emigrants decided to rest there another day. They had gained time by taking the cutoff trail and could afford to let their animals feed on the sweet valley grass for an extra twenty-four hours. Not everyone rested, however. Some blacksmith work was needed, and Dave had to pump the bellows for his father's forge. He didn't mind, except that Sol Jenkins and Larry Beeman were off fishing while he labored. Then Lucy came over to talk to him, and he forgot all about envying his friends. As usual, in the girl's presence he was tongue-tied, but she chattered fast enough for two.

"I hope we have some more dances," she said. "Don't you? You're good at it, Dave. Most of the other boys might as well have two left feet, but you seem to move right with the music. I could dance with you all night!"

Fortunately, there was nobody to hear her except Thomas March, and the burly blacksmith kept on hammering iron without a smile.

"Yeah, it was fun all right," said Dave, red-faced. "But I guess there won't be many more times when we aren't all tired out."

That was the last night they spent on the Green, and the wagon people turned in early. As Freeman Doane reminded them, they still had close to a thousand miles to travel, and according to all reports, the hardest part of the journey lay ahead.

Eleven

Water was less of a problem now that the train had reached the Green. Prudently, the movers filled their barrels after the crossing, but Jeff Barlow assured them there would be plenty of small streams on the next part of the trail.

Two hours after sunrise the wagons were lined out, climbing a dry, rocky ridge on the west bank of the river. Back in the dust rode Dave, herding the loose cattle along at the rear. His only companions were the old hound, Jupe, and a stocky Swedish boy named Arne Mortenson, who rode a flop-eared mule. Arne and his family had come down from Iowa to join the train. He was only a year older than Dave, but he wasn't very good company because he spoke only a few words of English.

The wagons had disappeared over the top of the hill when Dave heard a growl coming from Jupe's throat. Looking over his shoulder, he was startled to see half a dozen horsemen beyond the dust cloud made by the animals. They were coming up the slope at a gallop, crouched low over their ponies' necks, and he knew they were Indians.

"Arne!" he shouted. "Ride ahead an' bring the men—quick!"

As the young Swede lashed his mule, Dave hustled the straggling cattle into a run and pulled his rifle out of the scabbard, loading it hastily as he rode. The Indians had been silent so far, but now, as they drew nearer, they began to yell, and their piercing howls made Dave's blood run cold. He could see Arne riding far up the slope, but he knew the Swedish lad could never bring help in time.

Dave was desperate now. He pulled the snorting Cinder to a stop across the trail, raised his rifle, and took aim at the foremost rider. The brave saw him and swerved just as he fired.

For a moment the Indians reined in their ponies, seeming disconcerted by the shot. Then, bending so low they were hardly visible, they whipped their mounts into action again. This time, instead of coming straight toward the herd, they quartered to the left, galloping on a curving line that would bring them out above the cattle.

Dave kicked Cinder into motion and caught up with the last of the hurrying cows. Meanwhile, he was reloading his rifle as fast as he could. If the savages were going to kill him, he meant to take at least one of them with him.

By then the circling redskins were close to the top of the ridge and swinging over to cut off the herd. Poor Arne was right in their path, and he hauled the panting mule to a stop, waving his arms and crying out in terrified Swedish.

At that moment two riders came over the crest at a dead run. Both brandished rifles, and one let out such a piercing whoop that the Indians halted in confusion. Hardly believing the miracle of their arrival, Dave stared upward. One man,

he saw, was Jeff Barlow, and the other was his own father. They reined in beside young Mortenson, facing the raiding party. And after a brief hesitation, the leader of the Indians raised his arm in token of peace and walked his pony forward to parley.

Dave could hear Jeff speaking gruffly to the brave, piecing out the Indian words with sign language. Then the warrior replied in his own tongue. Jeff nodded, handed him a small deerskin sack of tobacco, and after another gesture of friendship, the six braves rode slowly off to the southward.

"You all right, boy?" Thomas March called to his son.

"All fine," said Dave. "But I was sure glad to see you. How'd you know to come?"

"Heard your shot," Jeff Barlow answered. "Your dad an' I were headed back this way anyhow, an' we just hurried it up a bit."

Dave drove the cattle ahead of him till he was able to talk without shouting. "Who were they?" he asked. "It looked to me as if they were about to run off the whole herd."

Jeff nodded. "That's what they aimed to do, I reckon. They're a bunch o' Paiutes from across the Uinta Range. They'll steal, but they're not much for fighting. I gave the head man a little present, just to show there were no hard feelings, but I told him all our men were dead shots an' they had itchy trigger fingers. He'll think twice before he bothers us again."

The sound of the shot had been heard by others, and several more men now appeared at the top of the hill. By the time Dave got to the last of the wagons, he was being hailed as the hero of the occasion, and nothing he could say seemed to change that opinion.

There was no danger of his getting cocky about it, however.

The first time he was alone with Jeff Barlow, the scout shook his head at him. "Just wondered if you knew how lucky it was you didn't hit that Injun," he said. "I reckon they wouldn't have taken it kindly. 'An' with your gun unloaded, it might ha' been all over 'fore we got there. As it was, they figured you were just trying to scare 'em a bit."

"What were Paiutes doing over here?" Dave asked.

"They told me they'd brought a few furs to trade at the rendezvous. After that, they probably followed the wagon tracks to see if they could steal some horses or cattle before heading home."

The train plowed on through more dust and heat and climbed more hills. In straightaway distance they covered only twelve miles that day, but as Dave's father remarked, they had traveled another dozen miles up and down. They camped by a nameless small stream, setting a strong guard over the cattle, and pushed ahead the next day to a river known as Smith's Fork.

The horses that pulled Callaways' wagons were nearly worn out by the time they reached that point. Most of the way to the South Pass, they had been grain-fed. Now the supply of oats was gone, and the animals had to live on such grass as they could find. The majority of the oxen, on the other hand, appeared to be in fair shape. Thomas March looked over his teams each night and seemed satisfied.

"A horse," he told his son, "gets to worryin' if the work's too hard or the feed drops off. He loses weight, an' first thing you know he's done for. But oxen, now, are different. They sort o' get used to rough goin' an' short rations. Look at old Duke, here. He's lean but he's tough, an' he never complains."

Dave liked to watch the four oxen when they were unyoked

at night. First, if they were near a stream, they went down to drink, two by two. Then, in leisurely fashion, they picked places to roll in the sand. And finally they plodded off to find a grazing spot. But whatever they did, munching grass or resting, they did it together. Duke was always at Prince's side, and Star stayed just as close to his yokemate, Bright. Whether it was a special friendship they had developed or simply that they were used to each other, he never could be sure.

That night at Smith's Fork, Jeff Barlow called the men together for a meeting. "We're getting close to the regular trail," he told them. "Most trains go 'round by Bridger's Fort an' come back north to the Bear, a little south o' here. We've saved a couple o' days by taking the cutoff, but some o' your horses are pretty near ready to drop. The grass isn't bad here, an' if you want to stay a few days to feed 'em up, that's for you to decide. There'll be other trains along soon, an' you might want to join up with them.

"On the other hand, you folks with ox teams need to keep moving if we're to get through the mountains an' reach the Columbia before there's snow in the passes. My judgment would be we'd better split the train."

The arguments were long and heated, but the men with ox-drawn wagons were in the majority, and they finally won out. The vote was to push ahead, leaving those who depended on horses to find their way later. Since Freeman Doane was one of these, he resigned from the captaincy in something of a huff.

"Don't blame me if you ox drivers get in trouble," he told them angrily. "Once we get our teams rested and tie up with a bigger train, we'll catch you before you get to Fort Hall. And when we do, you needn't expect us to slow down for you."

"We won't ask for any favors," Thomas March replied. "The main thing is to get to Oregon, an' let's hope we all make it."

Before they turned in for the night, the main body of movers took another vote, this time for a new train captain. Dave wasn't surprised when his father was elected. He must have shown his pride because the last thing Thomas March said that night was a warning.

"Don't you act big because I've got the job," he growled. "It's a thankless chore and a heavy load to carry. Maybe I can help get these folks to the Willamette, so I'll do my best. But I wish they'd picked somebody else."

In the morning the train, now consisting of only nine wagons, forded the river and assembled on the farther bank. It was a proud moment for Dave when his father's deep voice roared "Wagons, ho!" and set them in motion.

Their hearts were high that morning. The valley of the Bear was by all odds the loveliest country they had seen. Trees and knee-deep grass covered the slopes. Huckleberries and blackberries hung on bushes beside the trail, and it was hard to keep the younger children from stuffing themselves with the sweet fruit. But what appealed most to the men was the rich, dark earth. Frost and Mortenson were farmers, and they picked up handfuls of loam, clucking and exclaiming over it as if it were gold.

"Hope Oregon's half as good as this," Frost said solemnly. "If we weren't so all-fired far from any place, I'd be content to settle right here."

For a short distance, the trail ran level along the river, and since he wasn't needed as a guide, Jeff Barlow rode out into the woods to hunt. Dave wanted to go with him, but his father had ordered him to drive the oxen. Now that Thomas

March was captain, he felt his own place was riding in front of the wagons. He was perhaps a quarter of a mile ahead and hidden by the trees when Dave, walking beside the lead oxen, saw a huge, dark shape come out of the woods. It was a black bear, the biggest of its kind he had ever seen. It lifted its muzzle to sniff at the cattle, then ambled across the trail and disappeared into the brush, heading toward the river.

The oxen snorted and tossed their horns, but a flick of the whip started them on again. Nobody else had seen the bear, for the March wagon now had the lead position.

Soon the road roughened and began to climb a series of sharp little hills with gullies between. The teams strained into their yokes, planted their feet, and hauled the creaking wagons up the grades. Then, when they were over the top, brakes had to be set to keep the vehicles from running over the oxen. Once the drop was too steep for the brakes to hold, and all the men assembled at the top of the hill to let the wagons down with ropes. That took time, and the train made only fourteen miles before sundown.

Jeff Barlow came back about the time the supper fires were being started. He was afoot, leading his pony, with a big blacktail buck across the saddle. Dave wondered how the people they had left behind would make out without Jeff's rifle to supply them with meat.

"Sorry you weren't along today, boy," the scout told him. "Plenty o' game around—an' bears! Never saw so many bears. Black an' brown, all feeding in the berry patches."

"I saw one, too," said Dave. "A real big black one crossed the trail right in front o' my oxen. I guess whoever named this river the Bear must've found 'em as thick as you did."

Jeff nodded. "It's one sweet river, anyhow," he replied. "Too bad we can't stay with it all the way to Fort Hall. But we come to a sharp bend a couple o' days ahead, an' we'll have to cut north across some mighty rough country beyond Bear Springs. So make the most of it while we can, I say."

Some of the younger boys had caught trout that day, and all the families in the train dined well that night on fresh fish and venison. Mrs. March had even managed a blackberry pie for dessert.

The trail beside the river was better the next day, and they traveled in shade most of the way. The oxen had fed fat on the lush grass. Their sides had filled out a little, and to Dave's eyes at least, they looked strong and appeared contented when he unyoked them at the end of the haul.

Jeff Barlow came back from a long scouting trip northward and made his report to Thomas March. "There's a Shoshoni village camped by the trail, this side o' Bear Springs," he said. "Squaws, young 'uns, dogs—everything. They come over this way to hunt in the summer an' smoke their meat for the cold weather. I don't reckon we have to be afraid of 'em. It's not a war party. But just the same, we'll have to watch the stock pretty carefully an' keep our belongings inside the wagons."

The big blacksmith nodded and gave orders to each man in the train. He assigned his son to act as one of the cattle guards, warning him to fire in the air if he saw any Shoshonis sneaking around.

"All we want is to keep the herd safe," he explained. "Last thing we need is an Injun war. If we hear a shot, you'll have help in plenty."

The night was cool, and the breeze stirred in the pines overhead. As Dave sat there, he tried to remember what life had been like back in the Missouri village where he had lived so long. Probably, this time of night he'd have been curled up with a book or doing his school work. It all seemed hazy as a dream. The long, hard trail had become the only reality.

He kept awake through the first half of the night without seeing any marauders, and the second watch, after he was relieved, also passed peacefully. Hitching up the wagon the next morning, Dave wondered about the Indian camp. Jeff had described it as being some dozen miles ahead. If they could reach it at noon, they might hope to get to Bear Springs by nightfall. He uncoiled his whip and cracked it above the backs of the oxen. Like one animal, they leaned into their yokes and started to pull.

Twelve

Now that August was at hand, the full tide of summer lay over the valley of the Bear. The bushes were so filled with berries that they almost dripped with sweet juice. In the stream, trout that must have measured two feet in length were jumping after flies. And on far hillsides, the travelers could see little bands of deer browsing. All this abundance made Dave's mouth water, but he plodded on, keeping the wagon moving.

Noon came, and they still hadn't sighted the Shoshoni tepees. At Thomas March's order, the wagons pulled out in a little meadow beside the river, and the cook fires were started. The family had just finished eating and the tin plates were being gathered for washing when a noise reached them from down the trail, to the southeast.

"Horses comin' up this way," said Dave's father. "Wagons, too. Sounds like a lot of 'em."

Dave ran to look down the trail and saw dust rising in the distance. Then he could make out the shapes of horses moving at a trot and, behind them, the tall, swaying tops of prairie schooners. Whips cracked and teamsters yelled.

"It's a big train," he called to his father, "an' that looks like Callaways' wagons in the lead!"

In another moment all the movers were staring open-mouthed as the wagons swept past. They saw Freeman Doane behind his big black team near the front of the train, and he waved to them grandly.

"See you in Oregon," he called, "if you ever get there!"

The wagons whirled by—fifteen—eighteen—twenty of them—all pulled by four-horse teams. The animals still looked thin, but they responded to their drivers' whips and held the rapid pace.

When they were gone, Dave's father looked after them, his face grim. "Seems to me," he remarked, "some o' those nags don't look too strong, but they're makin' 'em move here where the goin's easy. You know it says in the Bible the race isn't always won by the swift. If I was a bettin' man, I might just put some money on our oxen to get there first."

They got on the trail again a few moments later. Thomas March told the drivers to keep their line closed up, and he sent several armed men to ride behind the loose stock.

"If there's any o' those Injun hunters in the woods," he explained, "they might be tempted to run off a horse or a few head o' cattle. So it won't hurt to play it safe."

Moving at their slow, steady pace, the wagons covered six more miles in a little less than three hours. It looked as if they might reach Bear Springs before dark, and Dave was wondering how soon they would sight the Indian camp when a shout came from behind him.

"Come back!" little Mr. Peck was wailing. "We lost a wheel!"

The wagons halted, and Thomas March rode by at a gallop, heading for the rear of the train. It was true enough. The left front wheel of the Pecks' rickety vehicle was lying beside the trail, and the corner of the tilted wagon rested on the ground.

"Pin sheered off," Mr. March reported, scowling, when he returned. "Help me get out the forge. We've got to make a new one."

When Dave was pumping at the bellows, his father explained. The cotter pin that went though a hole in the end of the axle had broken and fallen out, and the hub of the wheel had slipped off.

"That durn fool Peck," he fumed. "Never tars his wheels or he'd ha' seen something was wrong. Now we'll be held up here overnight, I reckon."

It took another hour to heat up the fire and hammer out a new iron pin. By the time it was finished, it was five o'clock, and there was nothing for it but to camp where they were. As darkness drew on, the blacksmith ordered the stock brought close to the wagons and appointed guards. But before they could take their places, Jeff Barlow rode down the trail.

"I doubt if the Shoshonis'll give us any trouble tonight," he said. "They've all left, bag an' baggage. From the tracks, I reckon they crossed the river. I stopped to say hello an' give 'em a deer for a present, but there was nothing left o' their camp."

"That's a funny one," said Dave's father. "What do you reckon spooked 'em?"

"No telling. They just left in a hurry, an' maybe we'll never know why."

The families had settled for the night and the younger children were asleep when three men rode into camp from the north. Dave recognized one as Freeman Doane, though the others were strangers. Hoarse with anger, Doane addressed the men around the campfire.

"We've been robbed!" he announced. "Right in broad daylight our spare horses disappeared. And the man who was supposed to be guarding 'em is gone, too."

"When did you find this out?" Jeff Barlow asked.

"Not till we got to the Springs. That was a couple of hours ago."

"Did you see any Injuns camped by the river?"

"They were there when we passed in the afternoon, but there's no sign of 'em now. Callaway and a dozen other men have set out to trail 'em and get the horses back."

Jeff shook his head pityingly. "Trying to chase Injuns in their own country is a good way to get killed," he said. "How many horses did you lose?"

"Around twenty, at least."

"Too bad," said Jeff. "But don't worry too much about the man that's missing. I'll see if I can find him."

The scout mounted his pinto and rode off northward, while Doane and his companions still fumed. They spent half an hour threatening what they would do to any Indians they saw from that time on. Then they returned to their own camp.

It was late that evening when Jeff came back. "Like I figured," he said, chuckling, "the Shoshonis hadn't hurt the guard. He was tied up in the woods just off the trail, gagged but able to make a little noise. If that posse hadn't been so all-fired anxious to kill Injuns, they'd have heard him moaning."

* * *

The movers spent a peaceful night and pushed on early the next morning. They all stared at the vacant space between the trail and the river, where the Indian camp had been. There were blackened ashes marking the locations of cook fires, but otherwise the place was clean and neat.

Two hours later the canvas-covered wagons of the other

train came into view. They were pulled into a tight circle as if to resist attack, and men with rifles kept watch, while the women and children stayed out of sight.

Thomas March and Jeff Barlow went over to talk to the men on guard.

"Did your posse get back any horses?" the blacksmith asked.

"They ain't back yet," a sulky teamster replied. "I see you folks have got a few horses in your loose herd. Want to sell 'em?"

"I reckon not," the wagon captain told him. "If you were real short o' teams an' couldn't move your rigs, we might lend you horses or steers, but we're not much interested in selling."

"Well, we ain't that desprit," the man answered. "I just thought some o' your folks might welcome some cash money. Ain't you feared of Injuns?"

"Not too much. We do keep an eye on our stock, though." And with that parting thrust, Thomas March waved the ox teams forward.

It was midday when they reached Bear Springs a short time later, and they decided to make an early camp. This was the last good grass they would find for a while, and it seemed a good chance to fatten up the oxen. Dave took his turn at guarding them, then went for a look at the springs themselves.

Half the children in the train were there ahead of him, drinking the fizzy water that came spouting out of the ground in several different places. It had a queer taste, like soda or sulfur, and if the youngsters' mothers had told them it was medicine, they'd have hated it. As it was, they couldn't seem to get enough.

The spring that fascinated Dave most was the famous "Steamboat." Its spout rose and fell with a roar and a hiss that sounded for all the world like the exhaust on a steam engine.

Even at night, as he lay in his blanket, he could hear the sound —a weird background to the howling of coyotes off in the forest.

In the morning the oxen were yoked and the water barrels filled at the river. There would be some dry, hard going on their way north to the Snake. The Bear bore away to the southwest and, so Jeff told them, flowed into the Great Salt Lake.

"Trains headed for California generally turn off here or at Fort Hall," he said. "They say there's desert beyond the lake, but it's no worse'n what we'll find on the way to Oregon. If I'm not mistaken, some o' those fancy folks like Callaway are likely to look at a map an' decide California's easier to reach."

Thomas March grunted. "Californy's all right, I guess," he said, "if you like to be governed by a passel o' Spaniards. I know the British lay claim to Oregon, but it's goin' to be American soon as enough of us settle there."

It would be a five-day trip to Fort Hall, the scout told them. And even that would depend on having no accidents to the wagons or the stock. But they set out with grim purpose, glad that at least their oxen were in reasonably good shape.

The trail itself was hard to find, for it climbed and dipped over bare black rocks. Only an occasional piece of a broken wheel or the bleached skull of a steer told them that other trains had passed that way before. It was hard country on the animals. Some of the oxen developed sore feet, and every night the forge had to be fired up to shoe them or repair worn-out tires.

Little clumps of grass grew among the ledges, but the horses and cattle had a hard time finding enough to keep up their strength. The people were little better off. The women and children had to climb the stony ridges on foot, often pushing behind the wagons or heaving on the spokes. The sun beat down on them, too, and the rocks were hot to their tired feet.

At night, even when the chill of evening descended on the high country, the rocks held the heat. Sleeping on the rocky ground under the wagon, Dave was grateful for the warmth that came through the blanket.

Each day Jeff Barlow rode in advance of the train, looking for easier ways to conquer their obstacles, and several times he advised taking a different route, to avoid sharp drops that would require letting the wagons down with ropes.

"Best day's work we ever did," Thomas March liked to tell his family, "was when we hired that artist feller for a guide."

By sheer grit and determination, they made it to Fort Hall by the end of the fifth day. The fort was a big, solid log building, standing in a clearing at a bend of the Snake River. Above it flew a flag—not the familiar Stars and Stripes but the Union Jack of England. It gave Dave a queer feeling to see it there. The banner brought home to him with a jolt the fact that they had left United States territory.

They circled the wagons at a little distance and drove the stock down to the river to drink. Meanwhile, a tall man in a scarlet uniform jacket came stalking out from the fort. He asked for the leader of the train, and when Thomas March stepped forward, he gave a stiff little bow.

"I am Captain Hunt," he said in a clipped British accent, "commanding this post of the Hudson's Bay Company. We're here to serve you in any way we can. Are there any sick people in your party?"

"Not as I know of," the blacksmith told him. "Thanks for

the welcome, anyhow. Maybe we'll have some trading to do, come morning."

"Gee," said Dave when the captain had gone, "he seemed friendly enough—as if he really wanted to help us."

Simon Frost had overheard the conversation. "Up to a p'int, I reckon," he said with a grin. "I've heard as how he gets pretty high prices in his store. No question he'd like to take in a few of our Yankee dollars, but I bet it gripes him to see us all swarmin' into Oregon. An' if we'd had sick folks, I doubt if we'd be so welcome."

There was a large fenced corral near the fort, empty at the moment. The movers herded their cattle and horses into it for the night, and all enjoyed a good sleep. Tired as they were, not a man of them was stirring before daybreak.

The boys were assigned to find better grazing for the stock and spent the morning riding herd. In the meantime, the women were at their eternal washing and mending, but they also enjoyed time to chat in the welcome shade by the river. Most of the men visited the trading post.

"Cap'n Hunt treated us right, sure enough," Dave's father reported at noon. "For those as wanted it, he set out good liquor—the first drink free. After that they paid, an' paid plenty. The prices aren't really too high, though, considering everything has to be brought overland, all the way from the Columbia. A barrel o' flour costs nigh three hundred dollars, an' sugar's forty cents a pound, so I reckon we'll try to get along on what we've got."

"I could use some cloth to make dresses for Patience an' Becky," Sarah March told him. "I'll go over this afternoon. Maybe calico comes a bit cheaper'n flour."

"Guess we can afford it anyhow," the blacksmith replied

with a grin. " 'Twon't take more'n a couple o' yards for such little tykes. By the way, one thing the cap'n sells cheap is horses. Fifteen dollars'll buy a fair animal. So Doane an' Callaway an' their bunch can stock up with spare horses once they get here. I reckon Hunt buys up broken-down nags from movers an' fattens 'em up enough to sell."

"I wonder if they ever caught those Injuns," Dave put in. "Seems as if their train ought to be here by now."

The words were hardly out of his mouth when old Jupe began to bark and they saw a dust cloud rising from the trail. Slowly, the wagon tops came into view, and then the riders. The teams were limping now, and their heads hung low—looking far different from the spirited horses that had passed with such a flourish a few days earlier.

The wagons dragged by and circled for camp, and after an hour or so Thomas March strolled over to see his former trainmates. When he returned, he shook his head in pity.

"They're pretty well beat," he told the others. "Fooled around for a whole day without finding hide nor hair o' their horses. Then one o' their men must've come on an Injun. They heard his rifle shot, but when they got there, the poor man had been scalped. Seems they had a rough trip over from Bear Springs, too, an' had to leave one busted wagon behind. 'Pears like hard luck just follows that crowd all the time."

Thirteen

One thing the horse-drawn train evidently had was plenty of money. They crowded into the trading post, sold their worn-out horses and bought somewhat better ones, drank a lot of the captain's whisky, and listened to the Englishmen and the bearded trappers discuss the terrors of the trail ahead.

After one of these sessions, Jeff Barlow came back to camp with a disgusted look. "We won't be bothered with that bunch the rest o' the way," he told Thomas March. "Those old mountain men would sell their own mothers for enough free liquor. What they're doing is trying to scare off movers from going on to Oregon. An' it looks as if Doane an' Callaway an' the rest are getting cold feet. One thing's true, o' course. Mighty few horse-drawn wagons could ever make it over that trail along the Snake."

Some of the ox drivers went to the fort to listen to these discussions, and Dave's father let the boy accompany him. Dave was impressed by the looks of the store. The shelves were neat and well stocked, and it was a much more businesslike place than the one he had seen at Fort Laramie. Grudgingly, he had to admit that the British knew how to run a trading post.

A bewhiskered old man in grease-blackened buckskins was holding forth to the assembled company.

"O' course," he was saying, "there's no law says you hafta go to Oregon. You take Californy, now. Land's so rich in that Sacramento valley, you stick sump'n in the ground, an' 'fore you know it, it's ten foot tall. Nice warm sunshine all the time, too. This chile figgers there's no purtier place on 'arth."

"How fur is it from here?" asked Skelly eagerly.

"Not too fur—closer'n the Willamette, anyhow. An' all nice, easy travelin'."

"Sounds good," Doane observed. "But I don't s'pose we could find a guide to Californy."

"Wal, now, that's funny you should mention it," replied the old mountain man with a leer. "I jest happen to be travelin' that way myself. Be glad to take ye down there an' won't overcharge ye, neither."

From where Dave sat, in the corner, he saw the old trapper wink at Captain Hunt. As Jeff had suggested, the British officer was doing all he could to steer emigrants away from Oregon.

That night, as the blacksmith was preparing to go to bed, Peck came sidling up. "Hiya, Mr. March," said the little man. "Thought I'd like to talk things over with you. I've about decided to go with the other train an' head for Californy. I thought Skelly'd come, too, but he says he'd rather stick with you."

"So?" March asked noncommittally. "You expect your oxen to keep up with their horses?"

"Nope. Cap'n Hunt'll take my steers an' milk cows in trade fer horses."

"Well, then," Dave's father told him, "I guess there's no more to be said. I wish you luck, but the rest of us are keeping on to Oregon. We'll be pulling out in the morning."

They were up at dawn. As he yoked up the oxen, Dave saw a gap in the little circle of wagons and realized that Peck had moved over to the other camp.

"Don't worry about it," said Jeff Barlow with a grin. "We'll be better off without his tribe. I doubt if that old rig o' Peck's could have made it, anyhow. We don't need numbers for safety any longer. From now on, what we need is stout wagons, good oxen, an' tough men. By the way, Finley, the storekeeper, has traded his horses for oxen, an' he'll put in with us."

Dave found it hard to believe that the way ahead would be bad when they set out that morning to the westward and left the fort behind. On their right, the Snake flowed sparkling in the sun or dark where the trees overhung it. The trail was broad and level, and the oxen stepped out willingly. At this rate, Dave thought, they could make twenty miles in a day.

It wasn't long, however, before he discovered differently. Craggy hills rose ahead, up which the wagons had to toil, and the river was lost to view, twisting through a canyon far below. The afternoon heat was stifling, and no breeze blew. Dust hung thick over the teams as they sweated and strained up the steep slopes. Then came rain on a chill north wind. The black rocks grew slippery and the footing treacherous. And the downpour, welcome at first because it cooled the air, soon soaked through their clothing and made the travelers shiver.

The wet-backed oxen struggled on, shouldering into the wind, but darkness came early, and they made only a dozen miles that day.

Jeff Barlow came by in the evening and found Dave huddled under a tarpaulin in the lee of the wagon.

"Cheer up, boy!" he said. "Only eight hundred more miles to Oregon City!"

Dave groaned. "Is it all as bad as this?" he asked. "Honest?"

"No, not all. Some's worse, o' course, but we'll see water an' green grass every once in a while. An' after we cross the mountains an' reach the Umatilla, things'll be easier. Don't fret—we'll make it before snow flies. Most of us, anyhow."

Sometime in the middle of the night, a man came hurrying through the storm to the Marches' wagon. It was Mr. Watson, a middle-aged schoolmaster from Indiana, and he asked Dave's mother to come quickly to see his wife. She had caught a bad chill, he said, and now was burning up with fever.

It was morning before Sarah March returned. She looked worn out by her vigil. "A mighty sick woman," Dave heard her tell his father. "We couldn't stop her shaking, an' if the fever don't break, I reckon there's no help for her. I wish we had a doctor along."

The train didn't move that day. The women folk took turns brewing herb tea, heating blankets, and sitting with the patient. But her temperature kept climbing, and she was delirious. The men got their own meals as best they could and stood around in discouraged groups, saying little.

Before darkness fell the rain stopped, and a pink sunset glow shone for a moment on the peaks to the westward. Then Mr. Watson climbed slowly from his wagon and came over to tell them his wife had died.

"Poor thing," he said brokenly. "She never was strong. I guess it was a mistake to bring her out here to this miserable country."

Two of the men dug the best grave they could by lantern light, and in the morning Mrs. Watson's frail body was laid to rest. There was no minister in the party, but Thomas March read some verses from the Bible, and they all repeated the Lord's Prayer. This was the first break in the ranks of the faithful Oregon-bound group. It depressed their spirits at the very time when courage was needed most.

For the first time, Dave found he was homesick for the easy ways of the East. There was a harshness about death in the wilderness that jarred him. Ever since the start in April, he had looked on this journey as an exciting adventure, but now it had become grim and unhappy.

As he drove, he watched the plodding oxen and wondered at their patience. There was no resentment in their sad eyes. They took the labor and discomfort and bore it without complaint. Observing them, he felt ashamed of his own sagging spirits. On to Oregon!

If anything, the trail was harder and more dangerous that day. Once they had to traverse a ledge only a few inches wider than the wagons, with a drop of hundreds of feet on their right and a sheer cliff going up on their left. The oxen crowded over as far from the edge as they could, squeezing Dave against the rock wall. His heart was in his mouth, but somehow they pulled the wagon through. The other vehicles also made it, and the frightened loose stock followed.

For those who dared to look down, the canyon of the Snake was an awesome sight. Far below—at least a thousand feet, Dave thought—the river boiled white over black, jagged rocks. The sound of it, lost in the distance, was little more than an angry murmur. It zigzagged this way and that like the serpent that had given it its name.

There were occasional patches of green down there by the river, and on the third day they found a steep track leading down to pasture and water. It was far too dangerous to take the wagons down, but the cattle were unyoked and somehow made the descent, scrambling among the rocks like goats. The only casualty was one elderly milk cow, which slipped and fell, breaking her leg so that she had to be destroyed. The cattle grazed and drank to their hearts' content. It was all the men could do to force them away and drive them up the path before nightfall.

The next evening the train rolled down a long hill to the banks of a smaller river that flowed in from the south. This, Jeff Barlow told them, was the Raft. Again the cattle and horses found good pasture, and there was plenty of driftwood for fires. Before dark they gathered on the bank to look at the fast-running stream. Jeff rode his pony in and found fair footing most of the way, though the last ten yards would require swimming the oxen.

Once more the men lashed logs to the sides of their wagons, and at dawn Dave drove the lead team into the water. He was riding Cinder at the left of the oxen—the upstream side—and held a rope tied around Star's horns. Halfway across, the black mare stumbled on a slippery rock and fell sidewise, throwing Dave into the river.

He kept his head and hung onto the lead rope, striking out strongly upstream. After a few anxious moments, he found his feet. Wading neck-deep, he held the oxen from veering with the current, and they made it to the other shore. Wet and fuming, he whipped them up the bank, recovered his uninjured pony, and rode back to help the others.

The Beeman wagon lost one of its floats in midstream and tipped over on its side. One of the bows supporting the top was smashed, so that a few pieces of furniture and a crate of hens were dumped into the current. The first job, however, was to haul Mrs. Beeman out of the water. Larry, Lucy, and Billy could all swim and thought the whole thing a lark. After the rescue the men of the train spent more than an hour recovering chairs and chickens from the eddies farther down.

"We're pretty lucky," Jeff Barlow told them. "I've heard o' trains that lost half their wagons an' stock crossing the Raft."

Two days later there was another, shallower stream to ford, and then came the long haul over the foothills to the Salmon Falls River. For four days and nights, they found no water, and Dave could count the knobby vertebrae along the backs of the oxen before they reached the river.

They had used the last drop from the water barrels. The view of green treetops by the stream brought a cheer from the parched throats of the movers, and the loose cattle in the rear got away from their herdsmen and ran bellowing down to the bank to drink.

Everybody in the party was too exhausted that night to do anything but sleep. Jeff Barlow assured them that, though there were many Indians in the area, the cattle were in no danger. In the morning they found out why this was so.

While the breakfast fires were being started, a dozen savages appeared out of the woods. They were fat and greasy-looking and wore nothing but ragged loincloths. Grinning stupidly, they offered to trade the salmon they were carrying with them.

The huge fish, fresh-caught, looked so tempting that they were soon bought up, the emigrants swapping cloth, beads, or fishhooks for them. That first day, after short rations on the trail, they all gorged on salmon and found it both delicious and filling. Jeff smiled to himself but said nothing to spoil their enjoyment.

To rest the animals and make a few needed repairs, the train spent all that day in camp. There were thousands of berry bushes nearby, and the children picked berries by the peck. Another thing the Salmon Falls Indians had to trade was a kind of cake, made from pressed, dried berries, and Sarah March prudently bought some of this for the journey that lay ahead.

There was a well-marked ford where the train crossed without mishap the next day, and before evening they reached the actual falls that gave the river its name. Dave could hear the rumble of the cataract long before the wagons drew near. It gained in volume until, when the falls came into view, people had to shout to make themselves heard.

The Snake came tumbling down a chute of black rocks and plunged into frothy turbulence below. But to the eyes of the Easterners, the astonishing thing was to see the great fish fighting their way upward through the falling water.

Naked Indians stood with nets in the eddies below and scooped the salmon up as they swam against the current. Over on the north side, a single huge grizzly bear was also fishing, using his mighty paws to flip the salmon up on shore. The savages paid no attention, and he, in turn, ignored them as long as they left him alone.

"Quite a sight, isn't it?" Jeff Barlow chuckled. "Plenty of

easy food for bears and Injuns. You wouldn't believe there were that many salmon in the world, let alone this one river!"

There was barely room to circle the wagons, there by the falls, and the stock found little grass. By bedtime, however, the movers had grown used to the noise, and they slept soundly lulled by the steady roar of falling water. In the morning, rising early, Dave wandered down to the Indian camp. A few squaws were stirring, but the men of the village, full-fed on salmon, still lay in their shoddy-looking wickiups.

These dwellings were built of sticks and rushes thrown together to form a half shelter, open on one side. And everything about the camp smelled sickeningly of decaying fish. Dave didn't wonder that the guide had such a low opinion of fish-eating Indians. They had forgotten how to hunt or fight and had grown fat and lazy with easy living.

The wagons set out again that day with water barrels filled, for there were thirty-five hard miles ahead before they could reach the crossing of the Snake. In dust and heat and over rocky trails, they made it in two days. Then came the long, steep descent to the river, with men holding the stop ropes behind every wagon.

Dave's first view of the crossing made his heart sink. The Snake had widened to nearly half a mile here, but it still looked deep and fast. In the middle was a long, narrow island, covered with grass and trees.

"The only good grazing's over there on the island," Jeff told the wagon captain. "Most trains swim the cattle over there to rest an' feed. You want to try it?"

"I reckon we should," Dave's father replied. "Let's unhitch an' drive 'em over. You, boy, take the yokes off the oxen an' get on your pony!"

Fourteen

The cattle rushed to the water to drink, but getting them across to the island was more difficult. The obedient Duke and Prince finally led the way under Dave's urging. They were able to keep their footing most of the way, and when they got within twenty yards of the island, they could smell the grass. From that point on, they swam eagerly for the shore. One pair after another followed quickly. Before dusk all the animals were grazing happily in their water-fenced pasture.

Once again the men went searching for driftwood logs, expecting they would have to buoy up the wagons. When they came back with nothing but small branches and brush, Dave's father began to wonder how they could make the crossing. As usual, it was Jeff Barlow who showed them what to do.

"Float logs won't work here, anyhow," he said. "The current's too fast, an' the wagons would all end up downstream. I've tested the bottom, though, an' it's fairly even—'round four or five feet deep all the way. What we've got to do is make the wagons heavy enough so they'll stay down. My idea would be to reload, putting the heavy things like cooking stoves an' plows on the wagon bed, then fill in with sticks an' brush, an' pile provisions an' perishable stuff on top, where the water won't reach 'em.

"If any of you don't have heavy ironware for ballast, use rocks. Goodness knows, there's plenty of 'em around."

Repacking the wagons was a long job, and there was some grumbling among the movers, but by midmorning all the wagons were ready. The Marches had no need for rocks, with all the weight of the anvil and forge and iron stock. Meanwhile, Dave and some of the other boys herded the animals back from the island, and the teams were yoked up.

Jeff's plan worked splendidly. Even in spots where the oxen had to swim, the wheels held the bottom. Men were assigned to stand in the neck-deep water and keep the wagons rolling, and by noon every one of them was on the island in mid-channel.

"Now," Jeff told them, "this second part'll be easier—not so far an' not so deep. Let's keep going."

Grabbing at mouthfuls of grass, the oxen pulled on across the island, then plunged into the river again for the final crossing. Riding alongside, Dave steadied the lead team and kept them moving. And almost before he knew it, the wagon was safe on the other side of the Snake!

They camped there for the night and made preparations for the hard overland journey to the Boise River. It would take four days or more, Jeff warned them, and the trail might get worse instead of better. It led through country fully as rough as any they had yet seen.

Many of the hills looked impossible, but Jeff went ahead, finding ways for the wagons to zigzag up the steep grades, or leaving the marked trail to pick a new and easier one. So they crawled forward, lucky if they covered ten miles between dawn and dark.

Dave's teeth were gritted with sand and his eyes reddened by blowing dust. Water rations were cut down to the point where his mouth was always parched. If he had been alone, he thought, he might have given up and turned back.

Then he would look into the dust-smeared, determined faces of his father and mother, striding beside the teams, and their courage bolstered his own. Some day, he told himself, there should be a monument erected to the brave men and women of the covered wagons—the movers who fought their way across plains and mountains, facing disaster day after day.

It was the middle of August now, and another worry was added to the load Thomas March already carried. Even if they reached Fort Boise in a week or ten days, there would still be more than two hundred miles to make across the Blue Mountains before they came to the Columbia. And they had all heard stories of September snows in the Blues, when the trail might be buried under ten-foot drifts.

One more day of heat and drought went by, and at last they came down into the valley of the Boise River. Water and grass had never looked so welcome.

In spite of the need for hurry that was becoming an obsession with the wagon captain, Jeff Barlow advised him to rest a day there by the river.

"You'll really be saving time," he said. "Worn-out teams can't get you across the Blues as fast as stout ones, an' right now some of 'em are so tired, they can hardly stand up. You'll be surprised how a day's good grazing an' plenty o' water can put new life in 'em."

Dave washed the grit off his body and had a good swim the

next morning. After that he spent a luxurious day lolling in the grass while he watched the hungry cattle graze. He had seen Jeff ride quietly out of camp in the early morning. The scout was gone all day, but when he returned toward evening, there was a blacktail doe across his saddlebow.

"Thought you folks might appreciate a change from those doggone fish," he said with a grin. "Game's pretty scarce, but I did manage to locate a little venison."

The journey down the Boise was easy compared to what had gone before. The trail ran near enough to the river so that good water was always within reach. There was decent pasture for the horses and cattle, and the slopes were easy, so that the women and children could ride instead of walking. One day they made an estimated twenty-five miles, which was close to the record. Jeff's advice about resting that first day at the river was paying off handsomely.

Moving steadily down the river trail, they reached Fort Boise on August 22. Nobody had been quite sure of the date till they checked it at the fort. The Hudson's Bay factor in charge of the post had a calendar on which he crossed off the days as they passed.

Fort Boise was a landmark that everyone on the train had looked forward to reaching, and now that they were there, they were disappointed. It was dirtier than Fort Hall and carried a poorer line of trade goods. That was probably because, instead of trading furs, the local Indians brought in nothing but dried salmon. The Scotsman who ran the place was barely civil to the Americans, and he sneered openly at their chances of getting through to Oregon.

Nearly all the space along the Boise and the Snake, which merged near the fort, was taken up with the racks of sticks used by the Indians to dry their fish in the sun.

"By gollies!" said the Swede, Mortenson. "Ay t'ought maybe we get away from fishes for a while! Dis smell, she's in my clothes—my hair—every place!"

Wrinkling his nose, Thomas March had to agree. "We won't stay here but the one night, anyhow," he said. "There's more hard trail ahead—a lot o' miles of it."

There were some repairs to be made to the wagons and a few staples to be bought. Then the train was ready to move. They made the second—and last—crossing of the Snake before dark and let the stock graze on the clean west bank, away from the Indians and their filthy-smelling salmon. Then everyone had a good night's sleep before the next day's ordeal.

The Snake ran through a deep gorge below Fort Boise, and there was no way for wagons to follow the river. So they struck off northwestward through hills that were covered with rocks and sand and sagebrush scrub. The oxen strained and the wagons jolted, while blazing August sun baked the skins of the travelers. The women wore their sunbonnets, trying to save their complexions, but the men and boys were long since tanned to a leathery brown.

Fifteen miles was the best they were able to do that day, but Jeff Barlow assured them that another effort as good as that would bring them to the Malheur River. "It's a Frenchified name that means something like 'bad hour,' " he said, "but don't let that scare you. It's good, clear water, not too hard to cross, an' there's grass there for the stock."

They made it by sundown, the second day out of Fort Boise, and as the scout had promised, the cattle found good pasture along the Malheur. That night Thomas March called the movers together for a council.

"It looks as if we're going to make it to the Columbia and

The Dalles," he told them. "I figured we could, or I'd never have taken the job as captain. But now we've got to start thinking about how we'll go on from The Dalles. A lot o' folks sell their cattle there an' go down to the mouth o' the Columbia in boats or on rafts. Myself, I hate to part with my teams. Seems like I'll have a lot o' use for 'em when we start clearing land an' hauling logs for a house."

"Why don't we take the wagons overland from The Dalles to Oregon City?" asked Mr. Beeman.

Jeff Barlow answered him. "Far as I've heard," he said, "it's hardly ever been done. Tried by some folks—yes. But they're dead an' buried some place in the Cascades. There's no more trail beside the Columbia than there is along the Snake. Horses an' cattle can make it, I'm told, but never wagons."

"We don't have to decide tonight," the blacksmith said. "But I wanted you to know the choices an' be thinking it over. I reckon none of us want to leave our household goods behind, so we'll have to be ready to rent boats or start building rafts as soon as we get to The Dalles. Then we'll decide who's to drive the cattle over."

Dave waited till the meeting broke up before he approached his father.

"I'd like to take 'em through, Dad," he said, "if there's anybody else to go with me."

The wagon captain looked him over thoughtfully. "It's a man's job," he replied. "But durn if I don't believe you're a man. Jeff says he'll do it, an' I reckon if anybody can see 'em through, he can."

"Gee!" said Dave, delighted. "Does that mean I can go? I'll sure feel better about the trip if Jeff's in charge!"

* * *

From the Malheur it took them two more days to reach the Brulé River—the Burnt River, as Jeff called it. And there the trail nearly broke their hearts. Some time in the past, a fire had swept the forest, and the growth that had sprung up was solid brush and brambles that hid earlier wagon tracks. Thorns ripped at the wagon tops as they tried to plow through. Men went ahead with axes and brush hooks to cut a path, but in some places it took more than an hour to advance a mile.

Where it was the worst, Dave had to ride the front seat instead of walking beside the oxen. And since his wagon led the way, it was up to Star and Bright to force their way through the thickets. The boy's heart swelled with pride for his team. The talk about selling them for beef was more than he could stand, and he vowed he would get them to the coast or die in the attempt.

To add to the discomfort of the train, great swarms of insects rose from the bushes as they went through. Mosquitoes and horn flies bit savagely at exposed skin, and even the horses and cattle were in torment.

Still they had not come to the worst part of that nightmare journey. The next day, after a dry camp, the brush thinned out a little. But now the trail led along the side of a steep slope where it seemed impossible for wagons to go. They stood there and stared at it in consternation.

"I don't believe it," Thomas March muttered.

Jeff laughed at him. "How do you think those wagon tracks got here?" he asked. "If any train can do it, this one can. What we'll have to do is put four or five men on the upper side of each wagon, with ropes tied to the boxes. I reckon that'll keep 'em from tipping over."

"All right," said the blacksmith dubiously. "If you're sure

there's no other way 'round, we'll try it. My wagon'll go first."

The women and children all got out and walked at the rear. Dave took his position on the left of the wheelers, struggling to keep his balance on the slope, and when he yelled at the lead team, the oxen lumbered forward. Every second he expected the heavy vehicle to tip, but his father and three other powerful men held tight to the ropes. After ten minutes of suspense, they reached fairly level ground on the other side.

"Come on, folks," shouted the wagon captain. "We'll take care of you! Just trust to the Lord an' the ropes."

One after another, the families traversed the slope, till only one patched-up wagon remained. That was the Skellys'. The hold ropes were made fast, and Skelly cracked his whip, yelling like an Indian. His skittish young steers plunged into the yokes and started almost at a run.

"Hold it!" March roared, but he was too late. The left front wheel hit a rock and lifted, and the frail wagon toppled down the hillside with a crash of breaking top bows.

Skelly stared at the wreck and broke into blubbering tears. The rest of the men stood awkwardly, pitying his weakness, but it was no use taking him to task. In silence they scrambled down the hill to pick up the scattered furniture and supplies.

"All right, now, Skelly," said Thomas March when he returned. "We'll tote your stuff across some way, an' I guess the wagon can be stuck together again. Just round up your stock an' keep your young 'uns out o' the way."

The train was stalled for two hours while the wagon was dragged up the hill by hand and repairs made on the spot.

"It don't look like much," the blacksmith commented, mopping his brow. "But I reckon it'll hold together for a while, anyhow—maybe even to The Dalles."

By luck they reached a little stream hidden in the brush just in time for supper. There was no fresh meat, but the movers made out with dried fish and corn bread, washed down with clear water from the creek. The mosquitoes buzzed about them in clouds, and all in all, it was a miserable night.

Two days of sweat and struggle got them through the Brulé, and the second evening the trail led down to Powder River. As if by magic, a northwest breeze started to blow down the valley, sweeping away the insects and cooling off the tired animals and people.

All the boys, including Dave, went downstream below the camp and had a swim. When he had dried himself and put on a clean shirt, Dave came back to the family fire.

"Feel better?" asked his father.

"I sure do. This afternoon I was pretty much licked, but now I could start for Oregon again this minute."

Sarah March smiled at him. "It takes a few knocks to make us appreciate the good things when they come," she said. "A sweet place like this restores a person's faith. Come on, you, Patience, an' you, Becky. It's time for bed."

Fifteen

Jeff Barlow left them as soon as they were across the Powder the next morning. He wanted to scout ahead, he said, as far as the Grande Ronde.

"Trail won't be too bad," he told them, "an' it's well enough marked so you won't get lost. Maybe, with a good day's pulling, you'll catch up with me at the Grande Ronde tonight."

When he was gone, the wagon master gave his call, and Dave cracked his whip over the lead oxen. After eating well they responded willingly, and the wagon rolled up the hill at a steady pace. Beyond, they came to more rocks and sand, more sagebrush and hot sun. But all the movers had a feeling that they had endured the worst the Oregon Trail could hand them. Perhaps now it would all be a downhill pull to the Columbia!

They took only a brief nooning—time to drink from the water barrels and gnaw on some dried salmon. Then they urged the cattle on again in the tracks left by earlier emigrants.

The Skellys' wagon rattled and swayed a good deal, but the fresh alder bows that had been cut and fitted at least held the ragged canvas in place.

They climbed the last hill about five o'clock, and at the top Dave gave a yell of victory. Below them for miles stretched a broad valley of woods and grassy glades. The cattle saw and smelled it, too, and began to step faster. In another twenty minutes, they were at the river.

Nothing Dave had been told could have prepared him for the Grande Ronde. To the tired travelers, it seemed like a kind of paradise. And as they stood there in the welcome shade exclaiming over it, Jeff Barlow came riding into camp with the body of an elk on his pack mule's back.

"Pretty, isn't it?" he asked with a grin. "An' there's game in the woods, besides. I'll try to keep you all in meat for a spell."

That night two Indians rode up with tanned deerskins to sell. Jeff said they were Cayuse Indians and had become Christians after attending Dr. Marcus Whitman's famous mission. Certain it was that they had been to school, for they spoke fairly good English. And also they were clean, with no fishy smell like the lazy savages of the Salmon Falls and the Boise.

Dave's cowhide boots were almost completely worn out, and he wanted moccasins like Jeff's. His father traded an ax head and some beads for a pair. They were well made, of tough elk hide, and a surprisingly good fit.

Off to the westward loomed the high ranges of the Blue Mountains, looking summery enough now. In another month they would be white with snow, but since the worst of the foothills lay safely behind, Thomas March felt less anxiety. He agreed it would do the train good to stay an extra day here on the Grande Ronde.

The decision delighted Dave, for it gave him a chance to go hunting with Jeff Barlow. The scout had spent the early morning sketching the circled wagons, the breakfast fires, and the women chatting over their washing, while the youngsters skipped stones on the placid river.

So sure was Jeff that they would find game, that he led the pack mule behind his pony. Together, he and Dave rode westward, up into the wooded hills. It wasn't until they were well out of sight of the camp that Dave heard a scrabbling sound on the rocks behind him and turned to see old Jupe following at a respectful distance.

"All right, old-timer." He laughed. "Come on—we'll let you hunt, too. Just try to keep quiet, so you won't scare the game."

They came to a little brook running down from their left. "You take this side an' go on up a way," Jeff said. "I'll cross over an' cover the right side. Ought to find a deer or two coming down to drink if we're lucky."

There was brush close to the stream, and Dave rode up into the woods, where it was clear of undergrowth. Cinder stepped along silently on the carpet of pine needles. The forest was quiet except for the distant chirping of birds.

Dave slipped his loaded rifle out of its scabbard and balanced it across his saddle, checking the priming. The hound had trotted past and was sniffing the ground ahead. Suddenly, Dave saw him stiffen and stand at attention, the hackles lifting along his neck and back.

"What is it, Jupe?" the boy whispered. "What do you smell?"

Then the pony must have caught the scent. He felt her tremble under him, and she tossed her head, refusing to go forward. The dog began to growl, deep in his throat. And the same sense of danger came to Dave as he stared ahead into the woods, gripping his rifle.

Perhaps it was Jupe's lifted head and steady growling that

made Dave look upward. There, on a limb a dozen feet from the ground, crouched a great tawny animal, teeth bared and tail twitching. So much he saw in one horrified glance. The next instant the huge cat launched itself at him, and Cinder shied to the right. That movement saved them both, for the beast landed just where the pony had been standing. Dave jerked his feet from the stirrups and sprang to the ground, still clutching his rifle. He would never have had time to shoot before the cougar's charge if the old hound hadn't roared in to attack.

There was a second's delay while the cat whirled, snarling, to demolish Jupe, and in that second Dave aimed and fired.

Luck was with him, for he might easily have hit the dog. Instead, his bullet sped true to the cougar's heart. It gave a bloodcurdling scream, bounded high in the air, and fell writhing on its side.

"Keep off, Jupe!" Dave yelled as the brave old hound made a rush toward the dying animal. The command was too late. One convulsive rake of the cat's claws laid Jupe's side open from shoulder to haunch, and he scrambled back with a whimper of pain.

Dave's hands were shaking, but he managed to reload the rifle. The cougar was still quivering spasmodically, and to make certain it was dead, he put another bullet through its brain. Then he sat down, panting and spent.

The reaction lasted only a moment, for poor Jupe came crawling to him for comfort, and he knew he must do something for his wounds. He got up, went to the frightened pony, and led her closer, speaking soothing words. Gently he lifted the old hound and laid him across the saddle.

Just then he heard Jeff's halloo from across the river, and he answered it. In a short time the scout appeared.

"Well!" said Jeff with a look at the big cat. "I heard two shots and the lion's yell, an' I sort o' figured you'd been in a fracas. You go ahead back to camp an' get the dog 'tended to. Leave the skinning to me."

Dave walked all the way, leading the pony, while Jupe lay still across the saddle, uttering only an occasional low moan. As soon as they reached the wagons, Dave called to his father. Together they lifted the injured dog down and laid him on a blanket.

"I'm 'fraid he's done for," the blacksmith said soberly. "Those claws went clear through the ribs, an' he's lost a heap o' blood. We'll put on some salve an' bandage him up, but you'd better be prepared for the worst. Don't take it too hard, boy. He was hurt doing what he liked best."

For the first time, Dave broke down. He had to fight to hold back the tears, for Jupe had been his companion almost since he could walk. When the dressing was in place, he sat beside the old hound and tried to make him comfortable. Jupe lapped a little water gratefully, then lay quiet again while his young master thought back over all the adventures they had had together.

After a while Jeff dropped by. He knelt at Jupe's side, and he could see the pain in the old dog's eyes.

"Poor fellow!" he murmured. "He sure was brave." And Jupe wagged his tail feebly.

"You think he's going to die?" Dave whispered.

"Maybe not. I know he'll make a good fight of it, anyhow. By the way, you killed some good meat when you shot that mountain lion. Some folks probably won't eat it, but the old-time trappers used to think cougar meat was better'n venison —or even buffalo!"

He was right about the movers' tastes. Only one woman was willing to try the stew Jeff prepared. That was Dave's mother, proud of her boy's accomplishment. To her surprise, she found the meat sweet and delicious, and Dave enjoyed some, too, though at first all he could think of was the hideous, snarling face of the big cat.

The animal's skin was sold to the Cayuse Indians the next morning. Then the train yoked up and started rolling again. Old Jupe rode in the back of the wagon instead of trotting alongside, and Dave sorely missed him.

When they stopped at noon, he took the dog some water and was pleased to see that Jupe could move his head more easily. His eyes looked less sorrowful, too, and his tail wagged with more authority.

That was the last day of August. After that it was a two-day haul across the foothills to the headwaters of the Umatilla. Where they first forded that river, it was little more than a brook flowing down through the woods. They camped beside it after the crossing, then struck out northwestward once more, to pick up the river twenty miles farther down. The Blues lay behind them now, but they still had some stiff climbing to do, over the northern slopes.

It was from the top of one such hill that Dave caught his first glimpse of great snowy peaks, far away to the west.

"Dad!" he cried. "Look yonder! Is that the Cascade Range?"

"I reckon so. How about it, Jeff?"

The scout grinned and nodded. "Sort o' hits you, doesn't it? That big one, off to the left, is Mount Hood—maybe two hundred miles from here in a beeline. Then, farther north, you can see Mount Saint Helens. And in between 'em, running all the way to Canada, are the Cascades. We'll be passing 'em mighty close on the way down from The Dalles."

Dave kept staring at the mountains as long as they were in sight. Then the trail dropped into a fold of the hills, and the distant peaks were gone.

* * *

The Umatilla had become a respectable stream when they came up with it again. And its very name made the hearts of the movers beat faster. As they followed its banks, the Umatilla would lead them all the way to the mighty Columbia itself—the river of all their dreams.

"Only a little more to go," the mothers would tell their

children. "We'll be building a house in Oregon 'fore you know it!"

There were no laggards among the movers now. They pushed the oxen hard, knowing there would be good water and pasture whenever they camped. All along the river, they seemed to be in prairie again, little different from what they had seen along the Platte so long ago. Cottonwoods grew along the banks, and grass and wild flowers abounded. Frost and Mortenson dug their fingers in the soil and wished they could put a plow in it, vowing they could raise bumper crops in a year.

Crops there were, already, for one evening some Indians appeared, carrying a big sack of potatoes to sell. The women snapped them up greedily, for their cook pots had been empty of potatoes for a long time.

The fourth of September was a red-letter day for the train. They had been moving downhill most of the morning, and shortly after noon everyone became aware of an earth-shaking rumble ahead of them.

"That's the river," said Jeff. "The old Columbia herself. She drops through a gorge a little way above here. We'll camp on the bank o' the Columbia tonight."

They whipped up the oxen and hurried on until the Umatilla flowed into a broad reach of water between dark hills. And there, overlooking the longed-for river, they stopped to sing a hymn of thanksgiving.

Thomas March came back to the wagon, a smile on his tired, bearded face. "Well, Sarah," he said, "we made it this far, anyhow. An' nothing's going to stop us 'twixt here an' the Willamette."

That was the spirit that pervaded the whole camp that

night. Only Jeff Barlow was inclined to be a little less optimistic.

"There's fresh wagon tracks here, less'n a day old," he said. "Another train, maybe a big one, is right ahead of us, an' that means all the boats may be taken by the time we get to The Dalles. Let's just hope you won't be held up there too long."

It was because of this warning that they rose before daylight and made an early start. A hundred miles lay between them and The Dalles—five or six days at the best speed they could hope to make.

As they soon discovered, the trail beside the big river was rough, with high hills to climb. Often the Columbia ran through gorges too deep to reach, and they made two dry camps before they came to the northward-flowing John Day River. They camped there, watering and feeding the stock, then went on through another long day to the Deschutes. And on the nearer bank of that good-sized river, they caught up with the wagon train they had been following.

It was a fairly large camp—forty wagons, Dave counted—and there seemed to be a vast herd of oxen and cows grazing along the shore. Jeff, riding ahead, held up a hand to stop the movers. Then, after speaking earnestly with Thomas March, he led the train upstream for another mile.

"The pasture'll be better here," he explained, "and I think the river's shallower, too—easier to cross. Maybe we can get the jump on those folks tomorrow morning."

They found a good campsite and turned the cattle out to feed. Some of the people in the train were disappointed. They had hoped to exchange news with fresh acquaintances or possibly find old friends in the other camp. But March ordered them to stay where they were and made it clear that their own welfare might depend on reaching The Dalles first.

It was a cold, clear night with a hint of possible frost before morning. Dave stood guard over the stock till midnight, and the stars overhead twinkled big and bright. September in Oregon was a beautiful time of year, he thought. And he was encouraged, too, by the way Jupe was recovering. The old hound was able to limp around now, and his scarred side was healing nicely. By the time they set out from The Dalles, he thought, the dog might be well enough to help drive the cattle.

Sixteen

He was awakened at dawn by his father's deep voice calling his followers to get up and pack the wagons. Breakfast was cooked and eaten in record time. Then the oxen were yoked, and the lead teams plunged into the ford. Jeff had found a good place for the crossing. Inside half an hour, they were heading across country toward the Columbia trail.

As they approached the big river, all the drivers looked eagerly to the right, wondering whether they had really stolen a march on the larger train. Then, seeing no wagons, a few began to think the other group might already have passed. It wasn't until Jeff returned from a scouting expedition that they were reassured. The trail, he reported, was empty for miles ahead. And they could be at The Dalles before night if they all stepped lively.

The Dalles! It was a strange name—French, maybe—and it had meant nothing to the emigrants back in the days before the trains had started. Now there was magic in it. And Dave, like all the rest, peered forward as he walked beside the oxen, hoping for a first glimpse of that promised land.

Late in the afternoon they came over the crest of a hill and saw The Dalles spread out before them. There was the trading post by the river and, near it, the low log buildings of the mission—a church and a school.

It wasn't quite as impressive as Dave had imagined, but it certainly looked busy. The cleared ground, back from the river, was crowded with more than a hundred wagons, their canvas tops ragged and dingy from the long overland trail. People, too, were swarming everywhere. Perhaps the March wagon train had beaten the one behind them, but a lot of others had arrived before. Thomas March frowned as he looked over the scene from the back of his horse.

"All right, folks," he called, "no need to circle your wagons, but keep 'em close together. You, Dave, when you've unyoked, hold the cattle in a bunch an' watch over 'em. I'll go see what's to be found in the way of boats."

Since the train would break up here, it was now every man for himself. The heads of families hurried down to the waterfront, hoping to find some way to transport their households down the river.

Jeff Barlow had already visited the trading post, and he returned now, just as Dave was taking the yoke off the wheel team.

"I figure you'll have some use for these cattle before long," he said. "They tell me there isn't a boat left, an' most o' these folks are cutting timber for rafts. But they've cleared away every tree for half a mile back. Your father'll need a raft, an' the logs'll have to be hauled from quite a distance. So, if I was you, I'd find good grass for the oxen an' get 'em well rested up for tomorrow."

This was excellent advice, but Dave soon found it wasn't easy to follow. All through that late summer and fall, thousands of cattle must have grazed along the river, and hardly a blade of grass was left. Leaving other boys to guard the herd, he finally drove the four oxen and the family cow back into a box canyon some distance from the camp and there found a spring, surrounded by good green grass.

It was there that his father located him an hour later. He was obviously angry because the boy hadn't followed his orders. But when he saw the pasturage and water, he didn't reprimand him.

"Reckon I forgot we weren't responsible for the other folks' cattle any more," he said. "Looks as if you'd used your head when you hunted out this place. Tomorrow we're going to have our hands full, cutting an' hauling timber. We'll build a big raft out o' logs an' floor it with the wagon beds an' side boards. Then, once we've loaded our goods, you an' Jeff can start overland with the stock."

"What about the animals that belong to the others?" Dave asked.

"Well, I guess most of 'em aim to sell to the trader. But Beeman wants to keep his. Says he's got a special strain o' good milk cows an' wants to start a dairy on the Willamette. He'd like to send a couple of his youngsters along with you to herd 'em."

Dave looked dubious. "Maybe they'll be all right," he said, "but neither o' the boys can shoot worth a darn. I was hoping Jeff an' I could do some hunting on the way."

"Hold on, now," said his father sternly. "You'll have just one job—to get the cattle through safe. An' from all I hear, it won't be easy. Larry Beeman's a good, steady boy. The other one's sort o' young, but I reckon he'll keep up."

"How's the rest o' the Beeman family plan to get down the river?" Dave asked, thinking of Lucy.

"They've asked to share the raft with us. Matter o' fact, it's a good idea to make it big enough for two families. An' I'll be glad to have another good man along to help me steer an' so on."

* * *

The next two days were filled with hard work for the Marches and Beemans. The men felled a dozen big trees and sawed them into twenty-foot lengths. Dave and Larry fastened chains to the logs, and the oxen dragged them all the way to the riverbank. Right at the edge of the water, the logs were laid side by side and the planking from the two big wagons made ready to put on top.

Instead of nailing the timber in place, the men used ropes and chains to hold the raft together. This was done on Jeff Barlow's advice.

"About halfway down," he said, "you'll come to the Cascade Falls. The boats are built to make it, but no raft can go through that white water, an' you'll have to take her apart an' carry around. There'll be Injuns there to help, an' they don't ask much pay."

At last the raft was ready. With rollers and pries, they inched it down into the river and moored it there while the household goods and farm and blacksmith implements were stowed amidships. Then came the provisions, and finally shelters were rigged at either end, using the canvas wagon tops.

When Thomas and Sarah March and the two little girls had been installed at the forward end, Dave waved good-by.

"You'll get there first," he called, "but don't worry about us. We'll see you in Oregon City as fast as we can make the cattle move."

He mounted his pony as the raft drifted out into the current, waved once more, and rode back to the place where Jeff was guarding the stock. It was then, as he approached, that he saw Lucy Beeman. She was dressed in boys' dungarees and a flannel shirt and mounted on a buckskin pony. A bedroll and provision bags were tied behind her saddle, and the butt of a shotgun protruded from a scabbard at her knee.

Dave reined Cinder in and sat there openmouthed. Then Larry Beeman rode up beside him, chuckling.

"I guess you thought Billy was goin'," he said. "But Lucy's a better rider, so she persuaded Pa an' Ma to let her make the trip. Don't look so worried. She can take care of herself."

Jeff Barlow wheeled his pinto and raised his arm. "All right, folks," he said with a grin. "Time to go."

In all there were nineteen animals in the herd they drove. These included two loose horses and Jeff's mule, which was actually packed with provisions and led, besides eight oxen and eight cows.

"There's no marked trail," Jeff told them, "so we'll just have to steer by the sun and the stars. We can go one of two ways—north o' Mount Hood or south of it. Either way the going's mighty rough, an' the distance is about the same—sixty or seventy miles. We don't have to make our choice until tomorrow, so let's go."

He rode off in the lead, heading westward through the woods, and the stock traveled after him. Dave and the two young Beemans brought up the rear, with Jupe trotting at the heels of the cattle.

"That's the dog that got hurt, isn't it?" Lucy asked. "He looks pretty healthy now."

"Yep," said Dave. "Old Jupe's been clawed by a grizzly an' then by a mountain lion. I reckon he's well enough to handle himself with any kind of animal we're likely to meet from here on."

"What do you think of my horse?" asked the girl. "Pa bought him yesterday from an Injun."

"Looks all right to me. A bit thin, maybe, but I reckon he's tough. Most buckskins are. Is he easy to handle?"

"Watch this," she replied, and guided the pony forward into a neat figure eight.

"Gee!" said Dave in honest admiration. "You *can* ride, sure enough!"

Soon they came to a series of bare, steep hills, sloping down toward the gorge of the Columbia. The cattle had to be urged up to the top of each one, then kept from stampeding down into the ravine on the other side. After four or five such climbs and descents, the riders and their charges were hot and tired.

"Just one more," Jeff promised, "an' we'll find water an' grass. Look—you can see the tops o' the trees in the next draw."

It had been well past noon when the little caravan started, and now sunset was approaching. When they reached the grassy stream at the bottom of the slope, the scout decided it was a good place to camp.

"We can turn the stock loose up yonder, where the pasture is," he said. "They won't stray if we're downstream because the canyon's too narrow."

They picketed the horses, and the two boys went up among the trees to get wood for a fire. As they neared the top of the ridge, Larry pointed westward and grabbed at Dave's arm.

"Golly!" he exclaimed. "Ain't that a sight!"

There against the sky reared the peak of Mount Hood, its snowy slopes tinged with pink. The mountain was so close and so vast that it took Dave's breath away. He was still star-

ing at the panorama when a shot rang out behind them, across the canyon.

"Hey!" cried Larry. "That wasn't Jeff Barlow—he went off to the south. Besides, it sounded more like a shotgun. You s'pose Lucy's in some kind o' trouble?"

The boys picked up their armfuls of wood and ran all the way down the hill. When they came in sight of the camp, there was Lucy, sitting on a rock and plucking the feathers from a large, plump bird.

"You'd better get the fire going," she said. "I shot us a sage hen for supper."

"Well, doggone your hide, sis!" Larry complained. "You like to scared us stiff. I figgered you shot off your gun to call us back."

Lucy grinned at him. "What sort o' trouble did you think I could get in?" she asked. "You don't expect me to miss a chance for meat in the pot, do you?"

Still grumbling, her brother piled dry sticks and tinder, and Dave produced flint and steel from his "possible sack." Within ten minutes they had a good fire going, and the bird, spitted on a green stick, was starting to roast over the flames.

Meanwhile, Lucy proceeded to mix dough for pan bread. When that was baking in the edge of the coals, she took a small pail and went off to the herd of cattle to get some milk. Only two of the cows were giving any at that time, but they needed to be milked night and morning. Also, it helped to have a little milk for drinking and cooking.

Just as the bird on the spit was brown enough to eat, Jeff Barlow came riding down the canyon. He got off the pinto and raised his hands, empty.

"Not even a deer track," he told the boys disgustedly. "But something smells mighty good. Who brought in the chicken?"

"Lucy did," said Larry. "Got a lucky shot, I guess."

Dave laughed. "I don't know," he said. "From what I've heard, she handles a gun better'n anybody in your family."

"Yeah? She's good enough, I guess, but I'm ready to shoot with her any time. All I meant was, she was lucky to see the hen."

The girl herself came back about then. She set her pail in the cold water at the edge of the stream and went to look at the biscuits in the pan.

"Everything's done," she announced. "Come an' get it. We'll have coffee later."

They all had good appetites. When Jeff had cleaned his tin plate, he grinned at the boys. "We're pretty lucky to have a cook like Lucy in camp," he remarked. "I'm free to admit her grub tastes better'n what I've been cooking for myself."

When the coffee had boiled and they sat around the fire, wrapped up against the evening chill, Jeff told them about his scouting trip that afternoon.

"I wanted to take a look at the country to the south," he said. "It's rough, all right, but I've got a hunch we'll make better time than if we try going to the north o' the mountain. Some places, I'm told, that trail is nothing but a goat track between the cliffs an' the Columbia. The south route may be a few miles farther, but I reckon it's safer. What do you say?"

"Well," said Dave, "I was sort o' hoping to see the boats an' rafts going down the river. But I'd rather trust your judgment."

"Me, too," said Larry Beeman.

"So would I," Lucy put in. "The main thing is to get our cattle to Oregon City in good shape."

"Very well, then," said the scout. "We'll try it. Either way we have to cross the Hood River, but it ought to be smaller an' easier to ford the farther up we go. Better turn in so we can make an early start tomorrow."

Lucy spread her bedroll next to her brother's, took off her boots, and rolled up in the blanket.

"Just like a boy," Dave thought approvingly. "She'll be all right on this trip."

As he was drifting off to sleep, a coyote howled back in the hills, and the horses snorted in the picket line. But Lucy lay quiet, undisturbed.

Seventeen

After they had traveled for an hour the next morning, Dave was glad the stock was well rested. Jeff had told them the country was rough, but that hardly expressed it. There were steep, punishing hillsides to climb, where scattered boulders and fallen trees made the trail almost impassable. Then it began to rain. The rocks grew slick, and one of the Beeman oxen slipped on a sloping ledge. It tried to get up and fell again, lowing pitifully. Jeff knelt and examined the animal's off foreleg.

"Broken," he said gruffly. "Bone's snapped just above the knee. What do you say, Larry?"

"Gosh!" the boy moaned. "Isn't there any way to save him?"

Jeff shook his head. "If we had two months to nurse him, maybe. But we have to be in Oregon City next week—remember?"

"Go ahead," said Lucy. "You know we have to do it, Larry."

She turned away, her eyes filled with tears, and put her

hands over her ears while Jeff and his rifle did what was necessary.

"I'm sure you wouldn't want any of the meat," the scout said quietly, "so we'll just be getting along."

Dave felt almost as bad as the Beemans. He couldn't help shuddering at the thought that the accident might have happened to old Duke—or Star—or Bright. How could he have faced his father after that? But he had to admire the courage with which Lucy Beeman took it. She was, he decided, a real pioneer woman, made of the same stuff as his mother.

The rain continued, and it grew colder as they climbed. There was no place to stop for a noon meal, so they chewed on jerked venison while they clawed their way upward. All of it was uphill now, and Dave thought they must be close to a mile high when they finally reached a long ridge, extending southward as far as the eye could see. To the north and west, the great bulk of Mount Hood was hidden in the clouds.

"It's snowing up there," Jeff told them. "We'll be lucky if we don't run into some drifts beyond."

"You mean there are more mountains to climb?" Dave asked, slatting the water off his slicker.

"Just a few. There's a big flat down yonder that we have to travel across first. Then we'll get into the rain forest farther on. You think you've seen some big trees? Wait till you're in among those firs and spruces!"

Darkness fell early that night. On the west side of the ridge, they finally came to a rocky outcrop that gave some shelter from the rain. And Dave found a low cave under the cliff, where it was possible to start a fire.

Lucy made a kind of stew out of jerky and dumplings, so that the four of them had a tastier meal than Dave would have expected. The animals were less fortunate. They found little pasture on the barren mountainside and stood there disconsolate with their tails to the storm.

Some time after midnight, Dave woke up shivering. The wind blew cold from the north, and with it came flying flakes of snow. He beat his arms as he went out to look at the cattle and horses. Their backs were white with snow, but they seemed to be all right otherwise. The fire had gone out, but he didn't try to relight it. Instead, he snuggled back into his blanket and pulled the slicker over his head.

When dawn came at last, they were stiff with cold, and the cattle were bellowing their distress. Jeff gave a series of crisp commands.

"Never mind breakfast," he said. "We've got to get the animals down to a lower level, out o' this snow. Pack up your gear, and let's get started. I'll lead the way to pick out a trail."

Within half an hour, they had descended a thousand feet or more and were out of the snow belt. Then the clouds broke, and the sun appeared over the ridge behind them. When they came to a patch of grass, Jeff ordered a halt.

"This'll give the cattle a chance to graze," he said, "while we eat some breakfast."

Warmed by hot coffee, they all began to feel better. Lucy milked her cows, and each of the boys had all the fresh, warm milk he could drink. Then, when the animals had snatched a few last mouthfuls of grass, the drive began once more.

The western slope was gentler and more gradual, so that there was less danger of slipping. Jeff led them down through a belt of aspen and birch to the broad, grassy meadows of the flats. They let the cattle move more slowly there, taking a little food as they went. Actually, Dave thought, the four big oxen of the March team seemed to be enjoying the trip. They wore no yokes and pulled no heavy loads, but as always they went together, Duke and Prince, Star and Bright, moving side by side. This, he told himself with a grin, was their first real vacation in a long, long time.

That afternoon their course brought them to the Hood River. Because of the rain, it ran high between its banks, fast and foaming.

"We might as well camp right here," said the scout. "Maybe the water'll be down a bit by morning. And there's a wonderful view of the mountain that I'd like to sketch. Why don't you hunt a bit, Dave? We could use fresh meat if you can find any."

"Go ahead," Larry put in. "Take sis with you if you'd like. Me—I'd rather see if there's any fish in the river."

He had already taken a hook and line from his saddlebag and was cutting a birch pole.

"What do you say, Lucy?" asked Dave. "I'd be glad o' some company."

"Sure," she agreed. "You want to ride or go afoot?"

"Let's ride. The game's easier to carry if we get any, an' we may have to travel a ways."

Jupe wanted to come with them, but the old dog was limping, and Dave ordered him to stay in camp. On the black pony and the buckskin, they went up the valley together. Where a stream flowed in from the left, they decided to follow it.

The sides grew steeper as they rode and the gorge narrower. After a mile or more, Lucy reached over to nudge Dave's arm.

"Look," she whispered. "There's a big brown bird in that tree ahead. I don't think it's a hawk. Let me try a shot."

She lifted her fowling piece quietly and took aim. At the

heavy bang of the shotgun, Dave saw brown feathers fly, and the bird tumbled to the ground.

"Pretty shot!" he said, complimenting her. "Let's hope it's something we can eat."

When they picked up the dead fowl, it was plump and heavy and looked a little like a prairie hen. "Well," said Lucy, "doesn't it look nice and edible?"

"Sure does," he told her. "Must weigh two or three pounds, too. We'll take it along and ask Jeff what it is."

He drew his rifle out of its sheath and made sure of the loading and priming. He hoped his skill as a hunter wouldn't be challenged by a mere girl.

As they advanced up the canyon, there was only a shelf of rock between the cliff and the river, and they rode in single file with Dave in the lead. He was guiding Cinder carefully, watching where she placed her feet, when he heard Lucy's voice, low and urgent.

"Look, Dave! Up there to the right!"

He reined in the pony and glanced upward. Two hundred feet above them, on a tiny ledge, stood a mountain sheep. He had never seen one before, but he had heard Jeff speak of the great curling horns. This must be a young ram or a ewe, for the horns made only half circles on either side of the head.

The animal seemed not to be afraid—merely curious. Slowly, Dave raised his rifle and took aim at the side, just behind the shoulder. When he squeezed the trigger, the report crashed and echoed in that narrow space. The sheep made a convulsive bound that took it away from the safety of the cliff. As the gray body fell, it bounced off the opposite side of the gorge, then turned over and over till it smashed against a big rock in the stream bed.

Dave was out of the saddle in an instant. He scrambled

down the canyon side and waded out to the rock, where the sheep lay broken and gasping. A merciful slash of his hunting knife put the poor beast out of its misery.

It was bigger than he had thought—almost as heavy as a blacktailed deer, he thought. All his strength was needed to carry the body to the bank, and if Lucy hadn't been there to help, he could never have lifted it up to the ledge where the ponies waited.

"That was a wonderful shot, Dave," the girl told him admiringly. "What is it, do you think? I can see plain enough it's not a deer."

"Bighorn sheep, I reckon. Looks like a young ram. Anyhow, the meat ought to be good."

They turned the surefooted ponies around on the ledge and threw the body of the sheep across Dave's saddle. Lucy rode ahead, and he followed on foot, leading the little black mare.

It was late in the day when they got back to their camp by the river. The cattle, fed to the full, were lying contentedly under the trees, chewing their cuds. Larry was cleaning half a dozen big trout, and Jeff was just putting away his drawing materials.

"Well! What you got there?" asked the scout.

"Just what I wanted to ask you," replied Dave with a grin. "My guess is it's a bighorn sheep."

"Right you are! A nice one, too. Here, I'll do the skinning while you boys start your fire."

"That's not all," said Dave. "Lucy shot a bird, but we don't know what to call it."

"Spruce partridge," Jeff told them. "They're fine eating. All of a sudden, it looks as if we're going to live high!"

* * *

With their stomachs full of fish, fowl, and meat, the four cattle drovers sat around their fire that night and discussed the country that lay ahead.

"I'd say," Jeff remarked, "that we've passed the worst of it. One more range of the Cascades to climb, but if the weather stays fair, it'll be easier than the last one. Then we'll come to the big woods. If we can find any sort of trail through the rain forest, we ought to make it to the Willamette in three or four more days. Tomorrow morning, though, we'd better smoke some o' that mountain mutton to give us meat along the way."

They all slept well. At daybreak Jeff rode off to scout the land ahead, while the Beemans and Dave built a fire of dry wood, added green limbs when it was going well, and hung strips of meat over it to dry in the smoke. The mutton smelled delicious while it was curing, and Dave was prouder than ever of the game he had shot.

They had eaten their noon meal before Jeff returned. He tried a piece of the smoked sheep and pronounced it sufficiently dry.

"We'd better get the cattle across the river now," he advised. "The clouds are building up again beyond the mountains, so we may get more rain before long."

They packed their utensils and provisions, herded the animals to the water's edge, and swam them across without much trouble. On the farther side, they started westward once more.

Within half a mile, they were climbing among the same kind of stony outcrops they had encountered on the earlier part of the journey. A sparsely wooded slope came next, then undulating brown plains, and finally, beyond them, what looked like a solid barrier of craggy mountains.

"You mean we've got to climb that?" Larry Beeman asked in dismay.

"After a fashion—yes," Jeff told him. "But it's not as bad as it looks. If we head around the shoulder o' that big cliff, we'll come to a sort o' pass between the peaks. No point in rushing, though. Those mountains are still twenty miles off."

They plodded on, crossing alternate ridges and high sandy flats. Ahead of them the mountains, which had seemed so near, remained at the same distance as far as they could tell. The clouds Jeff had mentioned now hung gray over their summits. There were no towering thunderclouds such as had warned them of summer storms back on the Platte. These clouds drifted mistily around the peaks, where it looked as if rain were already falling.

As the afternoon passed, the sun was obscured by the bank of gray haze, and miles still lay between the travelers and the mountain range.

"There's some shelter under those trees," Jeff said. "And from the way they're growing, in a line, I'd say we'll find water there. Let's make camp before the rain gets here."

They discovered Jeff was right. A little stream came down the draw where the cottonwoods grew. The scout rigged a small lean-to tent out of a tarpaulin and told Lucy to sleep there. The boys were supposed to be hardier and more used to sleeping under the open sky.

Lucy cooked them a good meal, and afterward they sat around the fire and talked.

"Here on the Pacific slope," said Jeff, "the rain sometimes doesn't come past the mountains. Could be we won't get wet at all tonight."

The Pacific slope! The words had a fine sound. "You

mean," said Dave, "that once we get through that pass, the ground'll slope all the way to the ocean?"

"Well, not quite. No more mountains between this range an' the Willamette, anyhow."

"Gee!" Larry exclaimed. "We *are* gettin' close, aren't we?"

"Jeff," Lucy asked, "who does Oregon really belong to—us or the British?"

Jeff chuckled. "Hard to tell, just yet. They got here first—or claim they did. But all they've ever really wanted was furs. So they've got trading posts all the way from Fort Vancouver to Fort Hall. But for every Englishman in Oregon right now, there must be twenty Yankees. Let 'em have the furs. What we want is to grow crops an' raise families on the good fertile land. It looks to me as if in another five years, there'll be so many Americans here they can't do much about it but allow our claims to the country."

"I'm glad," said Lucy. "We're going to live out here the rest of our lives, and I'd like to stay American."

The boys agreed with her heartily. When it was time to turn in, Dave took the first watch, knowing Jeff would relieve him at midnight. The sky was black enough over the mountain ridge, but right above him a few stars were twinkling. Jeff had said there was always plenty of rain along the coast, and Dave was glad of it. He remembered how midwestern farmers suffered in a drought.

Then he thought about his family, voyaging down the mighty Columbia on a homemade raft, and he sent up a silent prayer that they might make it safely. The thing he wanted most just then was to be reunited with his father and mother and his two little sisters.

Eighteen

Jeff came to stand guard about midnight, and Dave crawled into his blankets gratefully. It got cold, up there on the high plateau, in September. At dawn he was roused out again and hurried to help Larry build a fire.

"Got a long, tough day coming up," Jeff told them. "I'd like to be through the pass and into the woods by nightfall."

They got the herd started after a quick breakfast and set off along the shoulder of the high ridge. The weather had cleared, and as soon as the sun was well up, it got hot. Much of the way they traveled along sandy sidehills, so steep that the footing was bad.

"I had an uncle, lived in western Virginia," Larry told Dave. "He said the slopes were so bad, he had to breed a special kind o' cattle—short legs on the left an' long on the right. He called 'em sidehill cows."

"Yeah," said Dave, "I've heard the tale. Trouble was, he never could get 'em home again when they went out to pasture. If they turned around, they fell down."

"Serves you right, Larry," Lucy put in with a laugh. "You shouldn't tell such tall stories!"

They struggled on, up hills and down, with the ponies dripping sweat, the cattle lagging and tired. At noon the gap was in sight ahead—a sharp cleft between two mountains. They ate a dry lunch of jerked mutton while the cows and oxen browsed on such grass as they could find amid the sagebrush.

Two hours later they were crossing the saddle in the middle of the pass, then dropping down the western slope. Soon the rocks and dust were behind them. The tops of giant evergreens stretched away at their feet in an endless dark carpet. A little westerly breeze brought them a breath of coolness and a fragrant scent of pine.

"Doesn't it smell good?" said Lucy appreciatively. "Let's hurry down there."

The cattle seemed to feel the same way. They quickened their pace, sniffing the air from the woods, and a few minutes later the whole herd was in the shadowy coolness under the trees.

But if the forest had seemed like heaven to the hot and weary herders, they soon discovered it had its drawbacks. They had descended from the gap on a crude sort of trail that must have been used by other travelers in the past. But within a few hundred yards, it disappeared under a tangle of huge trunks, where dead trees had fallen or been blown down.

"Just hold 'em here," said Jeff. "I'll look for a way 'round."

The three younger members of the party sat their ponies and watched the restless cattle. Old Jupe sensibly lay down for a nap. Then, from nowhere, came swarms of mosquitoes, big and bloodthirsty. The cows and oxen switched their tails and shook their horns, the horses fidgeted, and the riders slapped at their attackers.

"Gosh!" Larry complained. "This is worse'n it was back

on the Brulé. You reckon we've got to fight bugs all the way to Oregon City?"

Jeff came back in time to answer his question. "I doubt it," he said. "They come from a swampy place just beyond here, but if we head around to the left, we'll be on higher ground. Let's get started."

He led them by a circuitous route till they were beyond the tangle of fallen trees and had firm footing under them. As if by a miracle, the hordes of mosquitoes disappeared. Only a few stragglers remained, too full of blood to fly away. The breeze came stronger from the west, and once more they found it pleasant among the huge trees.

There was no way to tell when sunset came, but before it grew too dark in the woods, they found a small, fast-flowing stream, swirling down between banks of huge ferns. It was a delightful spot for a camp, and there was plenty of dead wood with which to build a fire.

"Jeff," said Dave when they had finished supper, "how far do you figure it is now to the Willamette?"

The scout grinned. "Getting impatient, are you? If we don't run into any more trouble, I'd say three days. In all, it's not much over forty miles as the crow flies. 'Course, we're not crows, an' we can't travel in a straight line through the woods. We ought to reach the Clackamas River tomorrow or the next day. And once we're across, it's not very much farther to Oregon City—only a day or two, anyhow."

"It's funny, isn't it?" said Lucy. "I keep worrying about our families and how they're making out on their raft. And I expect Ma and Pa are just as worried about us. D'you think they'll be there ahead of us?"

"Oh, sure," Jeff told her. "The river moves faster an' steadier than we can. I've heard most o' the boats that come down from The Dalles make it to Fort Vancouver in two days—Oregon City in three."

"Well," the girl replied, "I hope you're right. I'll be awfully glad to see them, anyway."

Standing guard at night was now more necessary than ever, for if a cow strayed far in those thick woods, it would be nearly impossible to find her. Dave heard a lot of new sounds that night—not all made by things he could identify. There were no coyotes yapping, but a far more frightening voice came from the black shadows overhead. "*Hoo!*" it said. "*Hoo-hoo-ah!*"

When the echoes of the owl's cry had died away, the woods became full of small, scurrying noises. They were all around him, as if a whole army of furtive little animals was running for cover. Then there came an ominous creaking somewhere above him as the wind made two branches rub together. And through it all, he could hear the soft sighing of the evergreens. He could hardly help being homesick for the open spaces and the free prairie wind.

All of a sudden, his reverie was interrupted by a growl from the old hound. Dave sprang to his feet, listening. The forest was too dark for him to see anything, but he heard the cattle moving restlessly and the picketed horses snorting.

He gripped his rifle and held his breath as he listened. Off in the brush, a twig snapped, and Jupe growled louder.

"Who's there?" Dave roared at the top of his lungs. His yell had one effect—it brought Jeff hurrying toward him, and the scout had the presence of mind to snatch up a brand from the fire, now only a heap of smoldering embers.

Whirling the torch about him as he ran, Jeff brought it to a flame and held it high overhead.

"What was it?" he asked in a low voice.

"Don't know for sure, but it spooked the cattle," Dave told him. "Sounded heavy in the brush, like a bear—or a man."

Jeff stood still beside him and sniffed the air. "You get that fishy smell?" he whispered. Dave nodded, for he had noticed it at the same time. Jupe had stopped growling but remained on his feet, with his hackles up.

Once more they heard the crackle of a twig, this time from a good distance away.

"Well," said Jeff, "whatever it was, it's gone. And 'long as I'm up, I may as well take over the watch. We'll see if we can find any tracks in the morning."

When daylight came, Dave, Jeff, and Jupe went back into the woods together. Near the spot where Dave had heard the first noise, the old hound put his nose to the ground and moved eagerly southward. They followed him to the stream bank, and there, in the mud, was a moccasin track, ragged and splay-toed.

"Clackamas Injun," said Jeff laconically. "No wonder we smelled fish. They're a no-good tribe that hardly knows how to hunt. Live on salmon an' anything they can steal."

The two went back to eat Lucy's breakfast. Then the stock was rounded up, the duffel packed, and they pushed on through the forest. After half a mile, Jeff, riding in the lead, gave a shout of joy.

"There's a trail here, heading west!" he called. "This is what I've been hoping to find."

It wasn't much of a trail, but it showed many tracks of cattle and horses, and it had evidently been used less than a week before. Where trees were down, it skirted around them. In a few places axes had been used to cut through the brush, and the young herders were grateful to those who had gone ahead of them.

Following the trail, they made a steady three miles an hour all that morning. At noon they were in sight of the Clackamas River, and there they let the stock rest and graze.

Two Indians, fat and greasy, came wandering into camp while the party was eating. They wore nothing but ragged breechclouts and moccasins and silly grins. Lucy offered them stew and pan bread, but they refused, pointing to the large salmon one of them carried.

"No," said Jeff firmly. "No trade. No want fish."

The Indians acted surprised, then went off the way they had come, taking a long look at the herd.

"We'll have to keep a close guard tonight," Jeff remarked. "I wouldn't be surprised if they plan to follow us."

As soon as they had finished their meal, the scout rode his pony through the ford and announced that it was safe to cross. Except for a few yards near the farther bank, the cattle could wade, and they swam the short distance remaining.

On the other side, the marked trail continued. They kept the stock moving, trying to put as much distance as possible between them and the Indians along the river.

There were a few hills to climb, but none as rough or steep as they had had to conquer in crossing the Cascades. The cattle and horses moved eagerly, as if they knew they were on the way home. The broad Willamette Valley was close at hand now, and there were many little streams running westward through the forest.

Jeff halted the herd beside one of these brooks for a brief noonday rest. Then they were on the go again. The trail became wider, straighter, and more worn by travel.

"Look," Larry Beeman cried, "I bet we can reach Oregon City by dark. What say we get goin'."

Jeff grinned at him. "I haven't seen any mile posts," he replied, "but I'm beginning to think you're right. Let's try it, anyhow."

An hour later they saw an opening in the forest ahead. When they reached it, there was a clearing with fresh stumps and a small log cabin. Smoke was rising from its stick-and-mud chimney.

"Hello the house!" Jeff called, and a stalwart woman came out of the door.

"Howdy," she answered. "Reckon yo're headin' fer the river?"

"That's right. We're to meet the rest of our party at Oregon City. They came down by water from The Dalles."

She nodded. "Same thing we did. Only we sold our cattle. Had to pay double prices fer fresh 'uns when we got to the Willamette. How'd you make out comin' overland?"

"No special trouble. We lost one head, is all. How far do you call it from here to Oregon City?"

"Not more'n ten mile," she answered. "But don't try to make it 'fore nightfall. The road ain't too good. Why don't you stay here a spell? My man's back yonder, clearin' trees fer more land, but he'll agree. We don't git to see folks very often back here."

"You're mighty kind," Jeff told her. "But if it's only ten miles, I guess we'd better be going along. Any messages for the folks at the river?"

"Just tell anybody you see that the Danielses are gettin' settled in an' makin' out fine."

"Thanks, Mrs. Daniels," said the scout. "We'll do that an' glad to. Come on, you drovers—get the critters started."

Mrs. Daniels looked at them a moment. "Wait!" she called. "Ain't that a girl ridin' the yellow pony? What you doin' with her?"

Lucy laughed. "It's all right, ma'am," she said. "I'm well protected. This boy's my brother. Beeman's the name. We're along to look after my pa's cattle."

The woman in the cabin door still eyed them suspiciously as they drove the cattle out of the clearing and entered the forest again on the western side. Lucy continued to giggle for half a mile.

"I'd a lot rather sleep out, like we've been doing, than stay in that little log house," she said. "I'm sure she missed female company, an' she'd have kept me awake all night talking."

"Don't be so uppity about log cabins," Larry reminded her. "You'll be livin' in one yourself as quick as we can get it built."

They allowed no loitering among the cattle that afternoon. Dave rode at the rear of the procession, and his long bullwhip flicked the rump of any steer or cow that stopped for a nibble of grass. The trail continued good, and the animals kept up their fast pace.

As sundown approached, Jeff rode out ahead to see if they were anywhere near the settlement. He was certain they had come ten miles since leaving the Danielses' clearing. It was growing dusk in the woods when he came back.

"Doggone that woman," he grunted. "No idea o' distances. I went ahead a couple o' miles, an' still no sign of a town. Let's camp soon as we come to water. We can go on in the morning."

They found a stream shortly, and the boys made a fire for Lucy. She bustled about like a good housewife, getting out the food and the cooking utensils. And she sang a little song as she worked— "He said he would buy me a bit of blue ribbon to tie up my bonny brown hair." It went on through several verses, and Dave and Larry joined in the refrain— "Oh, dear, what can the matter be? Johnny's so long at the fair!"

Out there in the wilds, under the giant pines and firs, it had a homelike sound, and Dave began to realize home was close at hand. He ate his supper and took his rifle out to stand guard. This, he thought, might be the last time a guard would be needed.

He took a seat on a fallen log and watched the grazing cattle. The night was already black, and a mist was blowing in wetly from the west. He had never seen an ocean nor smelled one, but there was a salty scent on the wind, and he thrilled to the knowledge that the Pacific was there, only a matter of leagues from where he sat.

Nineteen

None of the party needed any urging to rise the next morning. By the time the sun was well up, they were on the trail again, plodding steadily westward.

At the end of an hour, they had covered about three miles, and Dave was beginning to wonder whether this trail really led to Oregon City when he heard a shout, up forward. Then, over the horns of the cattle, he saw a big bearded man on horseback. Jeff had turned his pinto and was riding toward them in company with the stranger. In the next instant, Dave knew it was no stranger but his own father!

Under his beard Thomas March was grinning broadly as he dismounted. "Good to see you all looking so healthy!" He chuckled. "An' Jeff says the critters are in good shape. We'd begun to worry about you just a mite."

"How'd the raft work?" Dave asked. "Are Ma an' the girls an' the Beemans all right?"

"All serene," his father answered. "We got held up a bit at the falls, but we got to Oregon City two days ago. Most o' the others got through, too. Finley was already in Oregon City when we pulled in, an' he's setting up his store. Frost an'

Mortenson have gone upriver lookin' for farmland. Come on—get the stock movin' now. We'll have dinner on the Willamette!"

They hurried the cattle along. When Jeff came back to help them, Dave rode up front beside his father.

"I was wondering," he said, "how Skelly made out coming down from The Dalles."

Thomas March's face sobered. "Poor Skelly!" he replied with a shake of his head. "He had a great plan. Sold his cattle an' bought three dugout canoes from the Injuns. Then he roped the canoes together, side by side, an' floored 'em over to make a raft. Everything worked fine as far as the Cascade Falls. He was tied up just above, unloading his gear, when the rope slipped. The raft was out in that fast water 'fore anybody saw it, an' a couple of his young 'uns, four or five years old, were still aboard. Skelly an' his wife just stood there an' saw the contraption smash to pieces on the rocks. They found the children's bodies next day, miles down the river. Most o' their goods were lost, too. What the poor things'll do now, I don't know. If I'd had a grain o' sense, I'd never ha' let 'em start the trip out here. Skelly's so beat now, I doubt if he can get up the gumption to start fresh."

This tragic news depressed Dave for a while, but he was too glad to be reunited with his father to dwell on it long. After another mile they came in sight of the cluster of frame and log houses and tents that made up Oregon City. In a matter of minutes, the young drovers had rejoined their families. Sarah March gathered her son to her in a bear-hug embrace that left him breathless, while Becky and Patience danced around him.

The Marches and Beemans were living in tents made from the old wagon covers while they waited for their cattle. But

Dave's mother had managed to set up a crude brick oven. In it she baked batch after batch of good crusty bread that was in great demand among the newly arrived travelers.

There must have been close to a thousand people gathered along the river, and more arrived each day. The town itself existed only to serve the new settlers, and all the buildings were as close to the riverbank as possible.

Dave was surprised at the size of the Willamette. It was a big river, slow-flowing, and it rose and fell with the tides. Many boats, propelled by oars and sails, were constantly coming or going, carrying supplies from Fort Vancouver and movers from The Dalles. And on the shore, half a dozen shops had been set up to deal in hardware, clothing, and groceries.

What struck Dave most forcibly was the sight of the flags that flew everywhere. For the first time since Fort Laramie, these were American flags! And the talk he heard around him was Yankee talk, without a single British accent. England might still claim the Oregon territory, but the people who were coming to settle it were Americans.

Before bedtime that night, Thomas March and his son had put the wagon frame together and attached the wheels that had been carried on the raft.

"There's a good enough trail leading up the river," his father told Dave. "What I want you to do is drive the oxen along the trail while we come by water. From all I hear, there's good land both sides o' the river for a long way south o' here. We'll try to keep within hail, an' if you see any place that'd make a good homestead, give us a holler. The way folks have been pouring in, though, I reckon it's all pretty much settled for quite a distance. Your ma and the girls can ride with you if they'd rather. We'll all get started at daylight."

* * *

The four big March oxen came willingly enough to the yoke when Dave called them. In fact, he thought they seemed glad to feel the familiar weight on their necks. They were in better flesh than they had been at the end of the long pull to The Dalles. The vacation had done them good.

The men stored the forge and other heavy equipment in the wagon, along with most of the furniture. Dave's mother chose to stay on the raft, with the Beemans and their goods, but Lucy and Larry accompanied Dave, driving their loose stock.

One hard wrench came when Jeff Barlow said good-by to them all that morning.

"I reckon I won't be much help from now on," he told them. "What I want to do is sketch the movers coming in here the next couple o' days. Then there's a ship sailing for Panama the end o' the week. I'll cross the Isthmus, get another ship to New Orleans, an' be back home in St. Louis before Christmas. There I'll paint pictures on canvas from my sketches.

"It's been a pleasure being with you all. I don't have to wish you luck because I know you'll take care o' yourselves in this fine new country."

Dave had an ache in his heart when he saw his friend ride off. But now there was a job to do.

"Hup, Star!" he called. "Get movin', Bright!" And he cracked the long blacksnake whip high over their backs.

The oxen settled into their yokes, and the heavy wagon creaked into motion on the southward trail. Out in the river, Dave could see the raft start at the same time, with his father and Mr. Beeman pushing at the sweeps. Lightened of much of its load, the unwieldy craft made fair progress against the slow-moving current of the Willamette.

Sometimes the wagon and the loose herd drew ahead—sometimes the raft gained, or even passed them. But in company they went on steadily all morning. There were times, of course, when the trail was hidden by woods from the river. Sooner or later, however, it ran close to the bank again, and the water-borne part of the expedition would come into sight.

When the sun was overhead at noon, the men guided their craft in for a landing. "Time for a rest!" Thomas March called. "Get us a fire started, an' your ma'll be ashore to cook up some vittles."

Dave and Larry brought the wood and lighted it. But before Sarah March could set foot on dry land, Lucy had gotten out the kettles and was starting to prepare a meal. Dave was amused to watch his mother's face.

"My lands, girl!" she exclaimed. "You're a quick one, an' no mistake."

"Who do you think did all the cooking on our cattle drive?" Dave asked. "Lucy's a better cook than most o' the grown-up women in the wagon train—an' a better shot than most o' the men!"

They made twenty miles up the river that day. As sunset neared, the blacksmith hailed his son from the raft.

"River makes a big bend to the west above here," he said, "an' the trail cuts off to the south. I reckon we'd better camp now because we'll be separated for a spell."

Dave unyoked the oxen, and they joined the rest of the cattle feeding on the lush grass. Soon the families came ashore for supper, and afterward they spent a pleasant hour around the fire.

"I've been noticing," said Mr. Beeman, "that the settlers

are thinning out a bit. This morning there was a cabin every quarter of a mile or so, but they're fewer now. I'd favor staking our claim before we get too far back in the wilderness. There's nothing wrong with this land right here."

"True enough," Thomas March agreed. "But I've sort of hankered to go a little farther up. They tell me there's a little settlement that's called Salem—after the town in Massachusetts, I reckon. If we took land near there, I could set up my forge an' get some business from the farmers around. Why don't we wait an' see how things look up that way? Ought to be there by tomorrow night, I figure."

To Dave, the name "Salem" had a romantic sound. He had read about the New England Salem, with its fine, tall clipper ships that traded around the world. Once they had made a home here in the Willamette Valley, he vowed to himself that he would go on west for a look at the ocean. Perhaps he would even get a glimpse of one of those big sailing ships, like the one that was taking Jeff Barlow to Panama.

The next morning, after the Beemans had agreed to go on for one more day, the wagon and the raft separated temporarily. The trail lay overland, cutting off the big bend in the river. For the most part, it led through woods, but often the young people saw newly built cabins and cleared ground, where men were burning stumps or plowing.

"Looks like hard work, don't it?" Larry observed. "I s'pose we've got to go through all that 'fore we can make a farm."

"What did you expect?" Lucy asked him tartly. "Hard work—sure. But it'll be *our* land an' *our* home!"

Dave pushed the oxen steadily, and at noon they saw the river once more. They pulled over to the bank, built a fire, and Lucy cooked a meal while they waited for the others to appear.

"They had more distance to travel," said Dave. "An' up this far there isn't much tide to help. They just have to buck the current all the way."

Nevertheless, by the time the food was ready, the raft came nosing in to shore.

"Come an' get it!" Lucy called proudly, and soon they were all praising her stew and pan bread.

"I've got so I like traveling on the river," Sarah March told them as she leaned back comfortably. "It's smoother'n riding a prairie schooner, an' you can sit back an' watch the scenery."

"Humph!" her husband snorted. "Just you handle one o' those big sweeps for an hour! Me—I'd rather let oxen do the work."

"Amen!" Mr. Beeman agreed with feeling. "We'll likely be all worn out before ever we get to homesteading!"

The trail stayed fairly close to the river that afternoon. About five o'clock Dave shouted to a man who was plowing between the stumps with a pair of horses.

"How far do you call it from here to Salem?" he asked.

The farmer grunted and spat before answering. "Too fur to git thar 'fore night—not with oxen anyhow. Might be 'round seven or eight mile."

Dave thanked him and ran over to the riverbank. After a moment the raft came into view around a bend. As it drew near enough, he called to his father and gave him the news about the distance to Salem. There was some discussion among the older members of the party, but they finally agreed to come ashore and camp. Only Mr. Beeman had his reservations. Going on to Salem, he thought, was a waste of time.

The next morning they were all up at daybreak, ready for an early start. The rowers manned their sweeps, and Dave whipped up the oxen. Behind the wagon where the loose stock were being herded, he could hear Lucy singing like a lark. And even old Jupe seemed to feel that they were nearing their goal. He trotted ahead of the caravan, spying out the land.

Back from the river were rolling hills, still covered by virgin timber. The hardwoods showed the bright orange and yellow foliage of fall, but most of the forest was the dark, rich green of pine and fir and spruce.

As they went on, more and more clearings appeared. A woman came out of a hillside cabin wearing a red calico dress, and though she was too far away to be heard, she waved a cheery greeting. Then, in the distance, Dave saw a gleam of white.

"There's the village!" he shouted. "We're getting close!"

* * *

The little settlement was hardly a year old; yet the people who lived there had made it look as neat and clean as a New England village. A tiny church, painted white, was at the center of the place. It was flanked by a general store and half a dozen homes, some of frame construction, some of logs. A small shack served as a lawyer's office, and it was there that homestead claims were recorded.

The Beemans filed on a hilly section about a mile from the village, where the soil looked right for good pasturage. Thomas March took a day longer to find the site he wanted. He chose a level area near the river, between two other homesteads and within walking distance of the Salem wharf.

"Got to be close enough so farmers coming to market can get their horses shod while they're in town," he explained to his son. "The land isn't so important, though this is good, rich earth. Next thing, we've got to get to work 'fore winter comes."

That night they were treated to some typical Oregon weather. A soft, steady rain came in from the sea and continued all night. The family slept in the wagon, as they had on the trail, and Dave kept fairly dry under the wagon bed.

In the morning he and his father went into the dripping woods to start clearing their ground. With freshly sharpened axes and a two-man saw, they brought the big trees down, trimmed the logs, and notched the ends so that they would fit together. It was hard work. Dave got blisters on his hands, then the blisters turned to calluses. But after the weather cleared, the work went faster. In four days they had logs enough for a decent cabin.

It was built a hundred feet back from the road, and the day they started putting it up, half a dozen neighbors came to help. One of them offered to build the hearth and chimney if they could get the stones together. That was Dave's job. He yoked up the oxen and hauled rocks from the river for two days.

At last the ridgepole was set, the pole-and-bark roof was in place, and the chimney built. The cabin had two rooms—a keeping room, where the cooking and eating were done, and a smaller bedroom. There was also a loft, in which Dave and the girls would sleep. Meanwhile, even before the house was done, they had put up a fenced corral and a lean-to shelter for the cattle and horses. A real barn would come next, and finally a log blacksmith shop at the roadside.

"Soon as the furniture's fixed up in the house," Thomas March told his family, "I reckon we'd better have a celebration. We'll invite the neighbors in an' give 'em cider an' doughnuts an' make it a real housewarmin'."

"Cider an' doughnuts!" his wife snorted. "I guess we can afford more'n that. If Dave can shoot us a deer, we'll have a barbecue. An' if he can't, we ought to buy a good fat pig. Look at all these folks have done to help us!"

Twenty

On the first day of November, the cabin was ready, and invitations had been sent out to all the people in and around the village.

Sarah March had been busy for days, cooking bread and pies. To Dave's delight, she had unpacked an American flag from one of the trunks they had brought from Missouri. That morning he cut a thirty-foot pole and set it up in the dooryard. When the halyards were attached, he stood proudly, watching the Stars and Stripes fluttering from the top of the pole.

The week before he had ridden his pony back into the hills and had been lucky enough to get a shot at a fine big buck deer. Skinned and cleaned, the venison had been allowed to hang. Now it was ready to be barbecued over a long pit, where a fire, carefully tended, was making a bed of red coals.

By ten o'clock the first guests began to arrive, and among them came the Beeman family. So far, Mr. Beeman told the Marches, his own cabin was hardly started. As soon as he and the boys had cleared a few acres, they had pulled and burned the stumps and plowed the ground.

"That's our corn field," he explained. "I don't aim to have to buy fodder for the cows next year, so I'm planting corn. We've been comfortable enough in tents, so far. Haven't lacked for meat, either. That gal o' mine brings home wild ducks every time she goes after 'em."

"They've been thick on the river," said Lucy, blushing. "You ought to try for some, Dave. There are so many, it's easy shooting."

"I've been sort o' busy," said Dave with a laugh. "But if you'll show me where to find the ducks, I'll try to get up extra early some morning an' go with you."

Nearly seventy people had arrived by noon, some coming by horse or ox cart from as much as ten miles away. One farmer, who had been several years in Oregon, brought a keg of cider. That was Thomas March's idea. He had heard the man raised good apples and had secretly arranged the matter.

"Far's the womenfolks are concerned," the apple grower told his host, "you can tell 'em this is sweet cider. It was, up till a few days ago, an' now it's sprangled just sufficient to put a little nip in the taste. 'Tain't hard enough to hurt a soul."

Sarah March saw the keg and chuckled. "Well, Pa, you got your wish," she said. "Just by chance, I had time to fry up a mess o' doughnuts while I was baking. They'll do for part o' the dessert, but there'll be plenty more to eat."

Fortunately, the barbecued buck was a big one, and there was enough meat to go around. In addition, there were potatoes baked in the ashes, fresh bread and butter, and more than a dozen big golden brown pies.

When all present had stuffed themselves, the men sat around talking land and politics, the women and girls cleaned up after the meal, and the boys adjourned to the river for a swim.

By four o'clock some had to start home to do their chores,

but before they left Mr. Beeman stood up and asked to be heard.

"I reckon all of us have been workin' hard to get settled," he said. "Maybe too hard. I hadn't realized how nice a holiday could be, an' I'm grateful to friend March, here, for askin' us. I vote we all give the Marches three cheers!"

The roar of "Hoorays" rang out with a will. Then somebody called for a speech from Thomas March. He got up, red-faced and reluctant.

"Those of you that know me," he rumbled, "know I'm not much of a talkin' man. I can make a lot better horseshoes than I can speeches. Just the same, there *is* somethin' I'd like to say."

He cleared his throat in embarrassment and hitched up his trousers.

"All the way out here, we movers kept hearin' how foolish we were to come to Oregon an' live under British rule. Every time we camped at one o' their forts, the Englishmen made it pretty clear they didn't hanker to have Yankee settlers movin' into their country. Well, we're here, spite of all. The way I see it, this Oregon country's too pretty *not* to be settled. All the British ever wanted here was a chance to buy furs cheap from the Injuns an' make money. They'd rather keep it wild, the way it is.

"But, friends, they can't stop the wagon trains any more'n I can stop the tide from comin' in. Pretty soon this valley is goin' to have thousands an' thousands o' people—all good farmers an' all good Americans. When that time comes, just by the force o' numbers an' the will o' the majority, Oregon's got to belong to the United States!"

He was answered by a swelling shout of approval, but he held up a big hand to show he wasn't finished yet.

"My boy Dave put up that pole yonder"—he pointed—"an' the flag that flies there is the American flag. If you want to give three cheers, give 'em to Old Glory!"

Again the voices rang loud. Dave, returning with the other swimmers from the river, heard the sound and wondered what it meant. It wasn't until most of the guests had gone that he learned what the cheering was about.

Lucy Beeman came and stood beside him, looking up at the flag. "You should have been here," she said. "I bet you never thought your father was an orator, but he made a speech about Oregon that had us all choked up. He really believes we've got to be part of the United States, an' he made us believe it, too."

Dave was proud to hear her say it. "I know," he told her soberly. "Pa don't talk a great deal, but when he does, folks listen. I believe him, too. I'll bet right now that before you an' I are old enough to have families, this'll be recognized as American territory."

"Good for you!" Lucy answered with a laugh. "Anyhow, I don't believe there are enough soldiers in England to keep us from singing 'Yankee Doodle' an' flying our own flag!"

Then she grew more serious. "Dave," she said, "how'd you like to be Governor of Oregon Territory? It could happen, you know."

It was his turn to chuckle. "I can't worry much about it just now," he replied. "There's too much to do—clearing an' building an' learning to raise crops. An' don't forget the hunting. If there's a frost tonight, the ducks ought to be flying, come morning. What do you say we go an' get some?"

When the Beemans had left, Dave wandered back to the fenced area where the cattle were comfortably chewing their

cuds. He called to the oxen by name, and all four of them moved close to the fence.

"Like it here, don't you, Duke?" he said conversationally. "All of you took a beating to get here, but I never heard you raise any fuss. Anyhow, those long, tough days on the trail are over. Not a thing to do now but haul logs an' plow an' eat, right here on the farm. Don't let anybody tell you Oregon isn't a fine place—for boys an' oxen, both!"

www.ingramcontent.com/pod-product-compliance
Lightning Source LLC
Chambersburg PA
CBHW020549310726
48979CB00008B/1147/J

* 9 7 8 1 9 3 1 1 7 7 7 2 6 *